TRUE NAVY
BLUE

A NOVELLA

SHARON HAMILTON

ISBN: 1517181925
ISBN-13: 9781517181925

AUTHOR'S NOTE

This is dedicated to all those who have loved once, twice, perhaps three times or more, and thought they should give up. I believe in Happily Ever Afters. I believe in long slow kisses and moonlit strolls on the beach. I believe in walks in the woods on sunny days. I believe in forgiveness and the healing power of true love.

Love hurts and makes us strong. I believe it brings us to the truest expression of ourselves, and when we strive for true love, we are striving for the very best within our souls.

Yes, even for Navy SEALs, *True Love Heals In The Gardens Of The Heart.*

Live well and love often. And let's explore the depths our hearts can take us, even in this very short ride of life.

authorsharonhamilton.com
sharonhamilton2001@gmail.com
Sonoma County, California
September 2015

CHAPTER 1

The red lights flashed, pulsing dangerous images across her white skin as she lay unconscious. Was she dead? He hoped not. Paramedics were pouring over her with care, asking hushed questions, obviously looking for some kind of response. And then, thank God, he heard her whisper something back and cry.

Where am I?

They were rougher with him. Zak Chambers was used to people around him making up their minds before they got to know him. Santa Rosa used to be a small town, back when his father was sowing *his* wild oats. Half the cops in town were kids of the same cops who used to arrest his dad for pranks he was legendary for doing—things like throwing pumpkins into the Redwood Motel pool at Halloween, making the headlines in the local newspaper. His father still had the article hanging on his garage wall.

And what was so wrong with pouring red Jell-O into the fountain at Santa Rosa High School? They were *his* high school colors and they'd just creamed Santa Rosa's football team 47 to 6.

Why am I thinking about all this stuff? Where the heck am I? What's happened?

This time, however, was no prank. His father's Camaro, a twisted and partially melted hulk in front of him, looked even more ghastly because of the red flashing lights, this was no prank. This wasn't about Jell-O or pumpkins or anything that could be construed as a high school caper. This was a first-class grown up tragedy, getting worse by the minute. He didn't have a clue what he was doing here or how he got here.

"Can you sit up, Chambers?" the gruff uniformed man with a badge and white plastic gloves asked him.

Where are the pretty nurses? His dad always got lucky with the nurses.

He tried to right himself, but the blow to his head had him confused. And he'd had a glass of wine, but just one…

"Need your permission to take a breath sample, son."

Fuck me. The guy looked younger than Zak did.

"No. Not going to happen," Zak mumbled.

"Oh, it's gonna happen. Either here or down at the station, but you better cooperate or you get an automatic suspension." The guy squinted. He had pimples. He looked like one of the boys he'd hassled in school.

"Do I know you?" Zak asked. The word "suspension" was rattling around in his head like a bad idea. He tried to focus on it, but nothing came.

"Oh yea, you do. You used to buy our booze with your fake I.D. when I was a freshman."

It was beginning to come back to him now. Little flashes of color. Painful things. Things he didn't want to remember.

"Except one time, you kept the money. You freakin' robbed us, man. Ain't life a bitch, Zak? Look at us now, dancing here on the pavement with your wrecked souped up Camaro your dad probably spent his year's pension on, and me here with my badge and gun and all. Oh yea, life is a real bitch sometimes."

Zak remembered him. Had an upper crust name like Dawson, or Drew or…

"I remember you, Dirtbag." It was what Zak always called him, not because he was a real dirtbag, because he worshiped Zak for the ladies he got to hang with. But it was given him because he was unlucky enough to be named Dirk by his parents. And Zak didn't want to be anybody's idol. He wasn't *that* fake. He just didn't deserve it. In those days, Zak was still a promising football player courting a couple of full ride college scholarships. He'd walked away from it all.

But what the hell am I doing here?

The kid administered the breathalizer and Zak saw the instrument yanked from the kid's hands.

"Still scoring points with the authorities, I see." An older man with a nasty gravelly voice and a nastier-looking face peered over the top of his head and blinked down at him, upside down. It made Zak dizzy. "And you're drunk," he said looking at the device. Instead of showing it to Zak he placed it in a plastic bag and shoved it in his large jacket pocket. "Works for me."

"Sir." Dirtbag stood up. "Should I test—"

"Yeah. He's drunk," the older officer said. "He needs to be taken in until we can figure it out."

It occurred to Zak he knew the man but couldn't remember his name.

When they stood him up, that's when Zak saw the other vehicle, a vegetable truck loaded with melons. Half of them were escaping over the freeway, bouncing like a girl's oversized tits with an agenda of their own. Cars were swerving and Zak expected to hear another crash any minute.

The older deputy barked some instructions. Two Highway Patrolmen took off with their lights flashing, while someone lit flares and started to direct traffic slowly in one narrow lane taking up part of the shoulder.

Ginger had not really been his date, but she was going to be his fuckbunny for the night, sure as shit. He'd made the mistake of letting her long lip lock go a little too long, distracting him enough to miss the overloaded melon truck swerving into his lane. The impact was on her side. As he heard it, he noticed the seatbelt firmly pressing into her chest, and like a dog, he had a second or two of turn-on before he realized they'd been hit.

Seatbelts were a good thing. In this instance, it probably saved Ginger's life.

"*He* hit *me*," Zak tried to protest as he was led, handcuffed, into the back of the patrol car. His shouts were falling on deaf ears as they closed the cruiser's door after shoving him into the rear seat. He saw the ambulance leave in a blaze of red and blue flashing lights ahead of him. He felt bad about not saying goodbye to Ginger before they took her away. He hoped she'd be okay.

The dark-skinned truck driver had a child clinging to his side. Zak noticed he wasn't being handcuffed and carted away like Zak was.

No, this wasn't going to wind up being a very good day.

The worst thing about getting taken down to the station was that his mother had to come down and pick him up. They'd not fingerprinted him or taken pictures, just put him in a cell with about twenty others, mostly drunk drivers, which made for a very uncomfortable sleep on a metal bench with a full-on fluorescent light buzzing overhead. But he didn't have time to tell her. She looked at him like road kill.

"I wasn't drinkin' Ma." He insisted. It was *almost* the truth.

"Zak, you're just one good time after another," she said, dragging on her electric cigarette.

"Where's Dad?"

"Sleeping. Right now that's a good thing."

He'd known that was the answer before he'd asked. He'd seen his dad down at the Irish Pub, rubbing shoulders with the computer nerds and yuppies who worked for Medtronic and Agilent. His dad was still better looking than he had a right to be, and though twice their age, could occasionally chat himself into someone's bed. Zak was glad he'd made it home. Now there was a *real* alcoholic, Zak thought.

"You know anything about Ginger?" he asked her.

"That the girl you were with last night?"

Zak nodded.

"News says she'll be released today. You're the one that needed the hospitalization."

He was relieved. "So that's where we're going?" he asked.

"They should have brought *you* to the Emergency Room. Dobson didn't do you any favors. He'd have probably let you bleed out, Zak."

Dobson. Holy fuck, Amy Dobson's father, the chief. He let her take a drag on her eCig.

"Can't believe it's your first day back and already you're in trouble. Surprised they didn't arrest you."

"They still could," he answered.

Now he began to remember. It was his day back only to attend his enlistment party a few of his friends were giving him. He was to report to Indoc in three days.

Thank God they didn't arrest me. This was way too close. Time to grow up and be smart if I want to really do this. His SEAL career would be over before it started.

Then he thought about his Dad's Camaro and was grateful he'd spent the night in jail. He had no idea what the old man was going to do when he woke up. Zak had completely blown his $65,000 ride. That cherry red beauty he kind of borrowed.

"I'll pay you guys back for whatever the insurance—"

She gave him a long horse-face look like he had a purple horn protruding from his forehead.

"I promise. I will, Mom."

"In your dreams lover boy." She sighed. "I never had to give this advice to your sister, so I might as well waste it on you. I hope you keep some rich little thing happy, Zak. If you can manage to unzip it for just one lady, you'd have a nice life making someone happy. I don't see it in you to be any kind of provider."

"I'm in the Navy now. Maybe I'll get killed and leave you the insurance policy, Ma."

She slapped him harder than he thought she was capable of.

"Word of advice. Stay away from the Amy Dobsons of the world, Zak. They'll make your life miserable, just like they always did."

Oh yes, now it was coming back to him. The fog was lifting. That summer when he was dodging classes and staying good and wet inside Amy Dobson's treasure chest. He'd fucked her so many times that year he thought perhaps his pecker would fall off. The girl was insatiable, used to multiple partners and always pushing the envelope faster than he could keep up. In the end, she tired of him and left him handcuffed naked to one of the oak trees outside the Admin building at Santa Rosa Junior College.

And then she called her dad, then Lieutenant Allister Dobson of the Santa Rosa PD, who got out his bolt cutters. He hesitated a moment, staring down at Zak's penis, swearing under his breath, halfway making Zak worry his pecker would be clipped. Dobson released him with a grunt. Zak couldn't help it if he was hung. Apparently that fact wasn't lost on her father, either.

He got off with a warning and he had to promise he'd leave town by the end of the summer. He was flunking out anyway. The scholarship was toast and his world was looking pretty small.

"Son, you either go away to college, or you go into the armed forces, or you hang out in Vegas with drag queens. Makes no difference to me. But Amy is off limits in a most permanent way."

No, Dobson, who had now made Chief, wouldn't do him any more favors. And now he didn't even get a chance to tell the Chief he was just passing through on his way to becoming one of America's finest. Probably wouldn't make any difference anyway.

They arrived at the Emergency clinic close to ten that morning. Zak's mother already had one message from his dad asking where the Camaro was.

It was going to be a very long day.

CHAPTER 2

Amy Dobson got a call from her friend Margrit at the Santa Rosa Police Department informing her that Zak had been held overnight. And he wasn't alone when he crashed his father's Camaro. He was with a girl.

Amy knew full well how much Zak's father loved that vehicle. But that's not what piqued her interest. She wanted to know about the passenger. Had Zak brought someone up with him to Santa Rosa? She'd followed his journey to Santa Cruz spying on him through Facebook. But this had come to an abrupt end when he joined the military. It was like Zak just dropped off the face of the earth with no posts on social media. Perhaps he'd blocked her.

She'd told herself whatever became of Zak was of no consequence to her. But it was an indisputable fact, when she was underneath some hulk of a guy who was trying his hardest to rock her world and cause the next earthquake, Zak's was the face she saw as she tried to get off. Back when they were dating heavily, all Zak had to do was look at her and her panties would get wet. He had more sex in his index finger than most the guys she knew would ever amass during their lifetime.

"Who is she, Margrit?" Amy knew the clerk wouldn't tell her, but she needed to ask anyway. She'd helped to get Margrit the job at her father's station.

"I'd have to go check—let me—"

"No. I'm good. Was she okay?" Amy wondered if the passenger was Zak's new girlfriend.

"Took her to Memorial. No serious injuries, and he didn't go to the hospital, if you want to know."

"You said that, Margrit. Said he was held over."

"And released to his mother this morning," Margrit said helpfully.

"Thanks."

Amy played with the screen on the phone, scrolling down through pictures. She and Zak at the ocean. She and Zak with selfies in bed. She and Zak completely shit-faced kissing in that photo booth at the fair the summer she turned eighteen, the legal age. Except that hadn't mattered to either one of them, since they'd been screwing since she was sixteen.

Even back then he was the only one who rang her chimes. He was the only one who didn't fall all over himself to get in her pants. She loved that he tried to exercise restraint, and in the end, he would always cave. That's the way he was. He was hers for as long as she wanted him, despite what he told himself, and despite whatever promises he'd made to some mystery woman who was in his car last night. Curiosity snaked its way up her spine as she wondered if he still felt the same way about her.

Rich Wilson, a new addition to her Dad's force, was coming over to take her to the Police Community Day at the park. Her dad would be there, of course, and she allowed Rich to curry favor with him by bringing his daughter to the party. She didn't like local cops as dates because they were more concerned about what her Dad was thinking than what Amy wanted, but today she would put up with Rich as a means to an end.

She fluffed her hair, adding some spray and fingering through it to add volume. Staring at herself in the mirror, she added a little extra eyeshadow and lip gloss over her red lip crayon. It was her reward for putting up with Rich. It made her feel a little naughty, wicked. Maybe Rich would get lucky tonight. What she really wanted was something else, but she refused to let herself dwell on it too much.

"You look awesome, Amy," Rich said on the front stoop of her father's house. He was attractive in his clean-cut way. He wore a dark polo shirt that hugged his nice torso. He wasn't huge, just well-built and took pride in how he looked. Eyeing him as she passed, she stepped out the door and let her heels clickety-clack down the concrete pathway, wondering why she couldn't fall for the really good guys. Oh yes, it could be a fun night, rocking his world, blowing his mind with some things she'd learned, but her appetite was tempered by the smell and feel of hot fresh sex with Zak. She couldn't help it if she was addicted to him. The taste of his kiss and the feel of his hands on her was still something she carried with her every day. It was like breathing.

Young cops in his father's Department always drove muscle cars or pickups with stick shifts. In either case, they didn't hold a candle to the souped-up Ford with the bench seat Zak had in high school. His dad had helped him restore it. She loved the smell of the old leather seats and the way the crackle of the radio sounded as they parked and watched the lights, as if trying to find their story out there amongst the strings of twinkling gold and silver. There wasn't any way to describe their relationship, really. They'd stare out at the jewel display, breathing hard, aware of the other, touching on that crackled leather seat. In the end the sirens always spooked him, as if her dad was sending a warning to him just before he did what he was no doubt going to do. She liked their little routine. Zak would protest, saying they shouldn't get so physical again, and, in the end he'd lose to Amy's persistence.

"We never talk," he'd said one time.

"Seriously? You want to talk? With me?" Amy let her eyebrows drift up into her bangs. "Do you know how many guys want to take a taste of these?" She had pulled her shirt up and when Zak tried to take just a discrete peek, it was all over. His hunger burst forth like an exploded water balloon. They couldn't get naked fast enough. Several times he fucked her before she could stop giggling at his urgency.

They never talked about what it meant. It was just assumed it was only sex, not a lifelong commitment. Back then, that was all it needed to be. As Amy looked outside her window, listening to Rich describe how awesome her father was and what a good leader and example he set for all the young recruits, Amy realized for the first time that she missed those carefree days. She considered, briefly, that perhaps it had meant something deeper, but then she brushed that consideration away like a dust bunny.

She let herself out of the car before Rich could get around to her side. "Dammit, Amy. I told you to let me get it."

"Oh, I'm sorry, Rich. I keep forgetting you are a gentleman. Just not used to it is all." She smiled up at him and she could almost see his buttons melt as his chest extended. She gave him her hand as a peace offering.

They walked across the bumpy lawn area that sometimes doubled as a Rugby field to the gathering of long tables covered in red and white checkered oilcloth. She heard her dad's gruff voice carry from the barbeque pit he usually manned, followed by several deep guffaws and some back slapping. He was a well-liked Chief, Amy noted, but he also had a temper and never forgot a betrayal, no matter how small. The respect he earned was more derived from his boundaries than his easy going nature.

Out of the corner of her eye, Amy saw that he'd noticed her arrival with Rich.

"Going to pay my respects to the Chief," Rich said to her ear as he gave her a little squeeze on her upper arms.

"Fine," she smiled back at the young policeman as she stifled a burst of irritation.

Margrit joined her. She'd come alone, as usual.

"Ginger Cooper. Not from here," Margrit said, her cheeks bunched like those of a hairless chipmunk stuffed with peanuts. For a second, Amy wasn't sure what she was referring to.

"Where's she from?"

"Listed an address in San Diego."

"Oh." It wasn't what Amy wanted to hear, finding out a girl from where Zak was stationed had come all the way up to give her competition. Amy knew she didn't have any claim on Zak, but if this stranger was something special to him, she needed to know, for her own edification.

"Jealous?" Margrit's horn-rimmed glasses and frizzy hair made her look dorky, like a librarian.

"Hardly."

Margrit sighed and looked over at the gene pool, most of them with wives and children. "You don't fool me a bit, Amy. You're as addicted to him as he is to you."

"Now you're talking nonsense," Amy said as she moved on.

CHAPTER 3

On the way home from the hospital, Zak's mother headed over to an attorney's office. Zak had kept mum all during the hospital visit, halfway expecting they'd get a call or the police would show up saying they were going to arrest him. His mom seemed to be on the same wavelength and mirrored his silence.

He'd needed this chance, and now perhaps it was all going to be taken away from him. After finally getting himself together, going through the Navy's basic training and an A school, he was finally allowed to try out for the Teams, something his recruiter had promised him. The Navy said they didn't know anything about that promise. When he tried to reach the recruiter, the guy was gone.

So he'd begged and insisted, passing up opportunities to go to Submarine School, based on his test scores which were the highest in the class. He didn't care. He wanted his shot at the SEALs. Finally his orders had come through after months of arguing and fighting with the bureaucracy. It would totally suck if today, because of one fuckin' going away party and a pissed off father of his ex-girlfriend, all of that was going to take away the one chance he had to turn his life around.

Weston Stark was a tall man, easily six-foot-five or so. He loomed over Zak and squeezed his hand like he was at an arm wrestling competition. The handshake hurt like hell.

"Congratulations, son." He motioned for the two of them to take a seat in front of his desk. Zak resisted the urge to flex and unflex his fingers to determine if any of them were broken.

"For what?" Zak shrugged as he lowered himself to the chair. "For ruining my father's car?" He could feel his cell buzzing from messages he'd not picked up.

"No. For enlisting in the Navy. Your mother is quite proud of you. I'm an old friend of hers from college years, you know." Weston gave a feral smile at Zak's mother while she stared down at her lap.

"Well, that must have been yesterday. I doubt today she's very proud of me now," Zack said, trying to get his mom's attention.

"So what line of work are you going for?" Weston was wound up tight, sitting on the edge of his desk, still looming over both Zak and his mother. His suspenders held up expensive dark blue suit trousers. He wore cufflinks, something that wasn't in Zak's wardrobe either.

"I'm starting BUD/S training next week. Qualification to become a SEAL."

"That right?" Stark let his eyebrows raise nearly to his hairline. "Wow. That's admirable. Best of luck with that. A tough course." He quickly glanced between the two of them, his mother still examining her fingers.

"Thanks."

"What made you decide to become, or at least try out for the Teams?"

Zak remembered the day he'd read the article about the kid from Petaluma who had become a Navy SEAL. Ten years ago he and Zak played on the same soccer team for a bit. The boy went on to distinguish himself, and then was killed on his last deployment. Something in Zak's DNA kicked in, and he realized it was time to go prove himself. Though living in Santa Cruz, he snuck up and attended the funeral, dodging local people who would recognize him. Their old coach was there, though. Coach Bardy gave Zak a heavy dose of reality.

"You're a fuckin' screw up, Zak. Had all the potential Joel had, and you just threw it all away." The coach was legendary for his in-your-face sidelines soccer dress-downs, when they were skinny kids just trying not to cry in front of all their teammates. It was what ultimately pushed Zak to football from soccer.

Bardy went on talking about his friend, the homegrown hero, and how Zak didn't have the balls to make it as an elite anything and would never measure up. As the man walked away, Zak was shaking in his shoes, fisting and unfisting his hands, tightening all the muscles in his upper torso. There and then, he decided, with the deepest conviction he'd ever had, that he'd live to make this man wrong.

Stark was still staring at him when Zak looked up. Even his mom was waiting for him to answer the question.

"Just something a man's got to do, I guess. My rite of passage." He carefully calmed his breathing, but his insides were boiling.

Stark crossed his arms over his flat abdomen and slowly nodded, like he expected a longer explanation. Zak had never told anyone about this decision, and wasn't about to do so today.

"Mr. Stark, thanks for your time, but am I going to need a lawyer, sir?" He held his breath for his answer.

"Good question." Stark said as he pointed his forefinger to Zak like a gun, winking his left eye. With surprising speed, he whipped around the desk to sit in his wine-colored leather chair. Zak sensed the man had been an athlete at one time. He methodically laced his fingers between each other as if it was an art form, resting his forearms on his leather blotter perfectly centered in the middle without any other adornment except for an old snowglobe of a Christmas scene. The globe was missing nearly a third of its liquid and seemed out of place in the office. When Zak focused on it, Stark picked it up and placed it on the credenza behind him like he'd left it out by mistake.

"You live under a lucky star, son." Stark used a lot of big words and said several sentences before Zak realized the likelihood of charges being pressed were minimal. "They could still come after you, but I have it on good authority they're not looking to cite you. I think holding you was just to shake you up a bit, to be perfectly honest."

He felt every muscle in his body relax with the relief that the accident wouldn't taint his chances for the SEAL training. That took the number three concern from Zak's mind. Number two was still the well-being of Ginger. His biggest worry was the confrontation that would in all likelihood take place today with his father.

"Seems your blood alcohol came back clean."

"I told them I wasn't drinking."

"The young woman you were with was way over the legal limit, poor thing." Zak saw the feigned sadness in Stark's face, like that of an undertaker.

"I'll bet." Zak also knew that was the only reason she'd agreed to go home with him. At first it had been so she wouldn't have to go home with one of his buddies who were all shitfaced. But after she kissed him and perhaps misinterpreted his meaning, he decided to go right along with the little charade and let the drama unfold.

"I think the fact that you were a Navy guy garnered you some points, son."

Thank God for a little break, at least.

"So like I said, your mother brought you in here to beg for me to represent you in what was looking like an ugly, ugly case." He emphasized *ugly* like the preachers he saw on television. The more time Zak spent around Stark the less he thought of him. The word "beg" stuck in his craw.

"Well, that truly is good news, then." Zak put his hand on his mother's shoulder and squeezed, silently asking her to look back at him. He was rewarded with a tired gaze followed up with a smile. The big elephant in the room was that there was still no cause for celebration.

"We even have a good Samaritan who came forward and said she witnessed everything, said the melon truck driver hit *you*. She's a security guard at the Junior College so she's a credible witness."

Stark leaned back in an arch, hands clasped behind his head, elbows out to the sides, looking as pleased as if he'd just told them they'd won the lottery and were millionaires.

Zak nodded. "Okay, then. All I have to do now is go see Dad. Might as well get this over with." Zak stood up and his mother popped up right beside him. Stark came to his feet and leaned over the desk to present a card.

"You make sure your father calls me in case he has any trouble with the insurance company. I have all the information about the woman who was the eye witness, and I'd be happy to share it with him, if he likes."

"Thank you," his mom said as she turned. Zak could tell she was trying to be polite, but when she took his arm, her fingers clutching his forearm, he could tell she wanted to get out of Dodge quick.

Zak held up Stark's card and waved goodbye. "Thanks for your time, sir," he said as he ushered his mother safely out of the office.

He helped her down the brick steps nearing the parked car. Zak finally found his voice. He was always careful with his mother's feelings. She was the only one in the family who supported and believed in him, but she was in a lonely crowd of one. "Geez, Mom, a friend from college? The guy's a shark."

"Was then too," she answered. "Don't ask."

"I just can't see—"

She stopped him before he could finish. "I said, don't ask. He's good at what he does and let's just leave it at that." She grabbed his arm and they continued to the car.

Zak started to chuckle. "Mom, you got a little bit of the bad boys in your blood, I see."

"I said, shut up."

But Zak could see the little quirk upward on her lips. She was about to smile and really didn't want to.

They drove to the Chambers' residence in silence. Just before they pulled up, Zak dialed Ginger's cell and got her voicemail.

"Hey there, Ginger. This is Zak. Just callin' to see if you're okay and all. I'm so sorry about last night. They told me you were released today, and I just wanted to check in. Give me a call, if you could."

He ignored the several other messages left by his friends. There would be time for that later on. He'd probably need their company soon, after his visit with his dad.

Zak saw a car door open across the street and noticed Amy Dobson walking toward him. He got out quickly, hearing his mother mumble something. She exited the car and proceeded up the walkway to their house ahead of him. Amy waved to her and got a brief return gesture as his mom continued to the house without even pausing.

His ex-girlfriend was looking attractive in a short black and white polka-dot dress with a neckline he usually liked, showing off her cleavage. He braced himself for an insult, but despite his internal alarm, his unit was reacting, just like every time he saw her. He sighed, but that didn't ease the tension in his body. He'd just dodged a bullet with the accident, and now Amy's presence threatened to drag him back into trouble. All his past poor decisions loomed. He didn't need another one.

She looked up at his bandaged forehead and briefly scanned below to the rest of his body.

"Hey Amy. Today's not a good day." He heard the front door slam shut, which distracted him until he looked back into Amy's eyes.

"I can see that, Zak. Glad to see you're not too hurt." She peered around him to examine the car. "Where's your girlfriend?"

"I don't have a girlfriend."

Amy nodded and stared at her red toes peeking out from high heeled sandals. When her head rose, their eyes connected like they always did, flaming something in his gut that wasn't healthy, like an itch he could never scratch. He gave up trying to analyze it. It was just chemistry.

He had the strength to step back. Zak knew it also wasn't fair to her. Why start something he couldn't finish? Besides, didn't she deserve more respect than that? He just needed to keep that up a little longer, and she'd be gone forever. "I'm just here for the day, headed back down to San Diego before I finish my training, Amy. I'm not back in town."

Her lip curled, and her left eye squinted. Zak looked away down the street trying to find something else to focus on.

"You have time to stop by my place later? I got a couple of things I wanted to discuss with you."

"Nothing to discuss, Amy." He was surprised his resolve was holding.

She rolled her head back, raising her eyebrows. "You never did like to talk much, Zak, but I kinda like it now."

"Well, that's a good thing then. Look, I've got to go. My folks are waiting. If I do anything tonight, it will be with Stan and Roger and the guys."

"And the little girl you brought up from San Diego?"

"I doubt that very much." He wasn't going to tell her she was Roger's little sister and had flown up to attend a family function.

"Love to see you in that uniform." She stepped closer to him but didn't touch. "Even better out of—"

He grabbed her wrists before she could lay her hands against his chest. "Amy, you got me all wrong. Those days are gone. I'm not that man anymore. I have a whole new life I'm going after, and I'm not interested in anything here. Anyone, either."

He released her wrists and watched as she stood before him with her mouth open, those red kissable lips gaping like she'd just seen a ghost. Her hands went down to her sides. He walked past her and up the steps to the front porch of his parents' house, never looking back.

CHAPTER 4

Amy raced back to work, arriving a full half hour late from lunch. Her boss wasn't back yet herself, so she was a bit relieved, but she'd stay the extra thirty minutes just in case anyone else was keeping score.

She knew where they would in all likelihood go tonight. Something told her that if she didn't see him one more time before he went off to the Navy, she'd never see him again. Amy wasn't sure why that was important. But it was.

In the two years since they'd graduated high school she had been restless. She should have gone away to college like so many of her friends had done. But she stayed behind and attended the Junior College, waiting.

For what?

With her mother gone, her father had wanted her to stay in the big house just so he wasn't alone, and at first she agreed. He was lonely after the long battle with cancer her mother had gone through all during Amy's high school, and she secretly hoped he'd start dating again. But his work seemed to occupy all of his time. He seemed to lose all interest in women, and began working such long hours she didn't know when to expect him home anymore.

Being picked up and dropped off at the Chief of Police's house was creating a major damper on her love life. But she didn't want to confront him about it, especially to tell him that. The new recruits on the force were safe for her, because they dared not act out of turn for fear of their jobs. But she wondered how much of their attention was just brownnosing and how much was serious.

She had a stack of brochures from some technical schools on the peninsula in Silicon Valley and San Francisco. That was more to her liking rather than being stuck in Santa Rosa. She was in the process of applying to them when she found out about Zak.

Were they just too young to get together? Was that the problem? God, how she wished she had something like a fantastic new job or some huge opportunity. But she had nothing except a healthy sex drive and a whole lot of history working that angle. Her reputation was legendary. For the first time in her life, she regretted not taking advantage of other choices some of her friends had made. She was being left behind.

She decided perhaps what she needed was just one more goodbye, and then she'd be done with Zak. Done with Sonoma County. She'd follow where her heart took her, move out of the house and start her new adventure. All she needed was a nice sendoff, and she knew Zak could do that. No strings. Just like the old days. Just a night of sex. And then forget about it until maybe some little high school reunion he probably wouldn't attend. He'd stand there, look at her, and she'd realize—whatever. All this stuff was foolish. She needed to get away from her father's circle of protection and out into the real world.

When she looked back at her life, there were lots of exciting days. But being with Zak made her feel like a woman. Had made her feel like a woman from the first time she'd kissed him. It was something she'd never allowed herself to admit until today.

So, this time, she'd just walk right into his arms with intention, and make the most of her last, carefree fling.

And then she'd grow up.

CHAPTER 5

Z ak's father was waiting at the kitchen table as his mother worked over the stove. He halfway expected his dad to come yelling out the front door, punching and fisting him, making a scene for all the neighbors. But the man he saw sitting there before him was calm, with murderous red eyes. Zak was more scared of him today than he ever had been.

He sat down and his mom handed him a beer, which he waved away. He noted his dad was drinking water.

"I'll take some ice water, Mom."

"So I got a call from my insurance agent this morning. That's when I heard you wrecked the Camaro. You wanna tell me, son, what you were fuckin' thinking borrowing a car *I* didn't even want to drive around last night?"

"I'm sorry, Pop. It was stupid. I should have asked you first. I wasn't gonna drink—"

"Drinkin's got nothing to do with it, Zak. *I* chose not to drive the car, because I was going to go out with friends. Some friends make you stupid. Especially *your* lowlife friends."

Zak bristled. His dad's assortment of friends weren't even allowed in his mother's house. Zak had known Roger and Stan for nearly ten years. But they still weren't saints.

"I'm going to pay you back, Dad. Every penny. I don't care how long it takes."

"That's not the point! The car was never yours to borrow." His father stood, his face bright red, and his ruby-colored eyes looked like they were about to burst. Veins at the sides of his neck pumped venom. Zak was concerned he'd have a heart attack. Even his mother came over and stood between him and his father.

"Jack. Stop it right now. This won't bring the car back, and you could do some serious damage to your health. Sit down. We need to talk about this."

His father piled his arms up over his head, sucked in air and screamed. "Goddammit, Zak. Why? How could you be so stupid?" When he lowered his arms, Zak could see he'd been crying.

Zak jumped up and hugged his father. The car had meant more to him than anything else he owned. How he wished he could bring back the last twenty-four hours and have a do-over. "By everything inside me, I'll get you another car. I'll help fix it up with you again, Dad. I'll pay you back every penny for all the parts, all the work done to it."

"You don't have that kind of money, son, and you never will." His father's arms pushed him away, shoulders lowered, face resigned. Zak's heart broke for the man.

"I don't care how long it takes. I'll pay you back. That's a promise." He said from the space between them.

His mother added, "Jack, at least Zak wasn't hurt, or we'd be sitting by a hospital bed. Don't forget that. The girl is okay as well. And from what I understand, this had nothing to do with drinking, either." Her stern gaze to her husband's eyes told him she meant business. "We have to keep things in perspective. Zak goes off to the Navy. We find out what happens with the insurance. We just hope they don't come back and find him at fault or charged with anything. That would restrict him from joining his SEAL training, right?"

Jack Chambers was still red. He listened, nodded his head. "I have to get away from here, or I'll say things to both of you I'll regret." His lined face looked painfully up to Zak. "This is way more beyond insurance, or the fuckin' money. It has to do with trust. I can't trust you anymore, Zak. I don't think I ever could!" His father turned on his heel and left the house.

His mother waited until her husband started the motor to their Toyota and sped down the street.

"I'm so sorry, Mom. I wish I'd thought about all this last night. I just didn't use my head. I'm going to work very hard to make sure those days are gone forever. Forever, Mom. I want to be the kind of son you can depend on."

"You already are. You have your whole life ahead of you. Jack will learn to get over it in time. I guess helping him is my job now. You go be with your friends, say your final goodbyes, and then you get out of this town and don't look back."

Stan and Roger met him at the brewpub. First thing he asked Roger was how his sister was. Zak ordered mineral water.

"Ginger's fine. She didn't even want to go to the hospital. But they thought she'd had a concussion. I guess she just got the wind knocked out of her, and yeah, she was pretty scared."

"I tried to leave her a message," said Zak.

"Yeah, she got it. She's going home tomorrow. Taking it easy at my folks today before she flies home. She's not mad. My mom is, though."

"I'll bet."

"Zak, it could have happened to anyone." Stan's upbeat voice didn't cheer Zak.

Zak thought about it for a minute. "I kissed her, Roger. Took my eyes off the road for one second, and that's when the truck hit her side. I'm so sorry, man."

"Yeah. She told me. Nice to hear it from you, though." Roger wasn't smiling.

"God, I've really fucked up, guys. I've got to change my ways. This is a wake-up call."

"We feel kind of responsible for inviting you up for the party. Some send-off this is. I wouldn't be able to live with myself if you'd done something to mess up your Navy gig, Zak," said Stan. "You were talking last night about Joel, and how you wanted to go do something like he did, be a hero, make something of your life, and look what happened. It would kill me if you messed up that chance."

"I think I'm more determined than before," said Zak.

"You know Joel very well?" Roger asked.

"Not since we were teens. Helluva soccer player. I don't know, he was a born leader. It's like we'd be down, he'd stand up straight, look into the sunlight almost, he'd say something inspirational and the guys on our team would just come together. We'd win against teams we had no right to win against. Never seen anyone like that before, or since."

"He liked you, too," said Stan.

"Yeah, he did. Tried to keep up with him through high school, though he was a year ahead of me. After he joined the Navy, I never heard from him again. Wish I had."

"He had a big influence on you. Never realized that until last night, the way you talked about him," said Roger.

"He's the reason I joined. No this, this thing I'm doing. It's exactly the right thing for me. I'm ready for this. I may not make it, but I could be a Navy guy. I just wanted to test my limits, you know, see how far I could go."

"You've got a lot more balls than I do. Gotta respect you for trying, Zak," said Roger.

"So you going back tomorrow?" Stan asked.

"Wish I could take off right now. But no, I think I gotta say goodbye to my folks one last time, maybe say goodbye to Ginger?" Zak looked up at Roger who looked like he'd chewed a sour lemon.

"Whoa! I wouldn't do that. She's fine. Besides, you can always look her up in San Diego later. She's okay. I'll give her your goodbye wishes. Just stay away from my folks."

Zak agreed. He stood. "Look, I'm going to head back home. Been a long couple of days, and I want to be rested for the drive back. Thanks, guys, for everything. Maybe the next celebration will be under better circumstances."

Zak took a last look at 4th Street, a street his father had driven up and down on Friday and Saturday nights in muscle cars back in the days when they'd go "tooling 4th" as they called it. He smiled when he thought about how happy his father must have been during those days. The way he talked about it made Zak feel like he was right there beside him the whole way. The destruction of the Camaro was more than about the car. He'd managed to eliminate the thin threads his father had to a cherished life now lost forever. He'd hold the heaviness, feel the weight of his guilt all throughout his training and maybe, just maybe, the hard physical work would pound it out of him. Maybe.

He heard a noise behind him. Turning, he saw Amy Dobson.

"Hello, Zak."

"Amy—I'm not in the mood—"

"Come on, Zak, it's been, what—nearly three years since we last spoke?"

"We spoke this afternoon, Amy."

"I mean, since we really talked. Can't you give me just five minutes of your time?" She held her fingers out, measuring, showing him how small five minutes would look, as if it was something she could hold. Her charm bracelet jingled and glinted in the night air. He'd made a lot of good decisions this afternoon and realizations about his future. He wasn't going to drink, he was going to go to bed early. He was going to head back to face his future and the biggest challenge he'd ever faced.

"Five minutes, Amy," he said as he held up his splayed fingers. Walking to his truck, he unlocked the passenger door, let Amy climb up inside, then walked around the front and sat behind the wheel. Night dew had formed droplets of water on the windshield, blurring car lights as they passed by.

Her scent came to him like it always did, at first itching his nose, then enveloping him in a familiar aura he'd lost himself in so many times over the years. The elixir of her just sitting beside him made his heart beat faster. His head cleared, pushing away the cobwebs of all the hurt and guilt he'd been feeling. A lightness came upon him. Was this how it was when a person was addicted to drugs? Did the anticipation of something that would take his mind off his problems give the addict a bit of clarity before the plunge downward?

And would this be a plunge downward? Was this good for him or bad for him? This was no celebration. The whole trip had become something entirely different than a celebration. It was like a tearing away of something, cutting the cord of something, eliminating his road back. Somehow, he knew that the man who would return after his BUD/S experience wouldn't be the same one he started the training with.

He dared a glance over to her. She slowly turned her eyes up to his. He could see the need in her face and her recognition that he'd also missed their times together. But, she didn't move, and neither did he.

"You once asked me why we never talked," she said carefully. Her eyes twinkled, and she moistened her lips. "Maybe it's about time we did. Just talk."

Zak saw she was trying to hide the smile forming on her left side, in spite of her efforts. That little twitch of her mouth spoke volumes.

"Is that what you want, Amy?"

"I wanted you to know that I'm proud of you, Zak. And I want to be here for you when you come home."

"What does that mean?"

"I'll wait for you."

"You? You never waited for anything in your life, Amy. I can't ask you to do that."

"I know you can't make any commitments, but I've changed. And what hasn't changed, I want to. I want to become the girl you come home to."

"No, that's not how it works. I can't offer you anything. Anything at all, Amy. I may never come back here. If I wash out of BUD/S, I might get sent off to the fleet and be gone for a year. I can't have you holding onto me. I just don't need that. It feels dishonest. I don't want to do that anymore. Do you understand?"

"Then trust me to wait for you? Trust me?"

Zak placed his palm against her cheek. One tear streamed down her face. "No, Amy. I can't ask that of you. I don't know where my head will be. I just have to focus on what's ahead. Please don't change anything for me. I'm not worth it. Really, I'm not." He could see it had finally sunk in. "Amy, we're going in two separate directions. We have two separate paths to follow."

She removed his hand from her face and held it in her lap. "Okay, Zak. Then let's just say goodbye nicely. Just one more time together and then we both go our separate ways. No strings. No agreements or commitments. Let's just part friends, good friends with a past we enjoyed together, okay? Can you do that?"

He did trust her, and it overrode his better judgment. Touching Amy had been a huge mistake. Now as her forefinger traced up and down his palm to his wrist and back again, the back of his hand against the fabric of her dress, feeling her thigh underneath, he could feel his resolve melting. He'd done so many things without thinking, it was new to be thinking carefully about whether or not to be with Amy one last time. She wanted it, he knew that. But damn, he wanted it too. Could he justify it as a way to say goodbye? Was it taking something from her to have a pleasurable encounter and then part? Was there dishonor in this, or was it a natural cycle, a final farewell to their relationship?

He smiled and cocked his head. "I think we've said more words tonight than we ever have had in the past."

She matched his grin. "I guess maybe we're growing up, Zak. I'm ready for a good old-fashioned grownup good-bye. How about you?"

"I think I can do that." He leaned over and kissed her. Amy let him lead and when she didn't pull him to her he wasn't sure at first if she really wanted him or not. But as her lips parted and she accepted him, as their kiss deepened, he could feel her fire burning, waiting to envelop both of them.

Her fingertips touched his face as they parted. Her brown eyes were honest, as tears continued to roll down her cheeks. "Thank you." She brushed back her cheeks and sighed. "You know where I'd like to go?"

"I think I do." Zak smiled back at her, turning to start the truck.

"You have a—" Amy looked over the seat to the small king cab seat behind them and found the familiar quilt folded there. "You still have it," she said as her face lit up.

Zak shrugged his shoulders, bringing his arm around her shoulders. "Part of my truck, I guess." Looking down the road he realized for the first time since he'd been home, he was relaxed and actually looking forward to the next few minutes with her.

CHAPTER 6

Oak trees arched overhead just like they always did, but Amy saw in their shadows a greeting, as if they were welcoming her home. She'd been to the golf course many times during the daytime over the past couple of years, even recently, but this was their favorite spot. She loved the smell of the fresh cut lawn, the sound of the night birds, how the stars twinkled so brightly, away from nearby harsh lighting.

Zak even parked in the spot he always parked before, at the end of the first row, turning off the motor. Headlights illuminated the course in the distance, rising and falling in swales and hills dancing in the shadows.

"You sure about this?" he asked her.

Amy knew the answer, squeezing his hand. "Yes. Completely." But she still felt a little scared even though her heart was beating with anticipation.

For the first time ever, she wanted him to know how much she'd missed him. What if it felt different? What if that luxurious chemistry they had was gone? What if they didn't have that spark, that feedburner of passion usually enveloping them? Would it still be okay?

He led her out from his side of the truck. They walked hand in hand, his left arm cradling the comforter. Frogs from the numerous creeks nearby abruptly stopped as they walked closer to their hiding places. She heard an owl overhead.

"Sure hope the sprinklers are turned off," Zak chuckled in reference to one of the times they'd been sprayed with water in the middle of having sex. She'd forgotten about that time, and it brought a smile to her face.

Zak lay the blanket down and sat. Amy took up her place next to him.

"This is the last thing in the world I thought I'd be doing tonight," Zak said.

"It's like, well," Amy hesitated, but continued, "I've thought about what it would be like to be with you one more time. I've thought so much about it, I kind of don't know how to act."

"Come here."

His kiss put her right back where she belonged. He smelled like the man she knew growing up. The feel of his cheek against hers, the taste on his lips was all what she'd remembered, dreamt about.

His hand slipped up under the hem of her dress as he stroked her backside. Amy leaned into him as he lay back, allowing her to ride his thigh. His fingers snagged her panties and slipped them down one side while she helped with the other, pushing herself against the length of his upper leg when she was free of her undergarment. She unbuttoned his jeans, and her fingers found him just as she always had. Squeezing his package she helped him ease his pants down over his hips with her other hand. He pushed her back against the blanket, hiking up her dress.

He dug into his pockets, fumbling a little and produced a foil packet. She took it from him, opened it and sheathed it over him. "I always loved this part," she whispered to him.

"Are we sure what we're doing here?" he asked.

"Ask me if I'm ever sure about anything, Zak. Are you?"

She felt and tasted some nervousness from him as they kissed. Before long, the heat came up between them and she was gasping for air. She noticed his breathing had shortened. His hands were smoothing over her breasts, her shoulders, her back and up the long ridge of her thigh.

He pressed himself against her opening and waited. Bending down to kiss her again, he said, "Amy, you know this is goodbye, right? I just want to be sure you are okay with us this way."

She smiled as he pressed, beginning to breach her opening, agreeing with him. "Why, what were you thinking?" She raised her knee, allowing him to slide inside. Looking into each other's eyes, he entered fully to the hilt. His thumbs smoothed over her cheeks. He dipped his head down as their lips barely touched for a couple of tender, soft nibbles. She grabbed the back of his neck, pulling him down and deepening his kiss. She arched, first to accept him fully and then releasing as their familiar rhythm began to pulse. His hot breath in her ear, the kisses he covered her neck with, the way he lifted her buttocks up and hiked her knees above him urgently telling her of his need ignited the fire in her soul.

He let out a small groan as his breath hitched. She pressed her chest against his, feeling the strength of his heart beating against hers, loving the feel that her arms could not fully encircle him. Her hands moved up and down the bulging muscles of his back. She held his hips as he undulated into her, pressing himself up and deep inside her.

Her natural instincts were to be urgent with him, but she let the rhythm build between them, long and slow, each coming together and parting approaching that oneness they used to feel as they made love. She never wanted it to end.

Already her body was spasming to his penetration, her muscles milking him. The familiar tingling sensation began spreading all over her body. Her spine became warm and liquid. Her knees hugged his sides as her legs crossed over his back. His rough kiss matched the urgent cry coming from deep inside his chest as he stilled, arched and she felt the familiar pulsing of his buried cock.

"Oh, Zak. Not yet."

"I can't help it, Amy. Ah! So sorry."

She found herself laughing lightly, snuggling with him as he kissed her chest, laughing too. "Oh, I remember this. I remember how wonderful I felt afterwards," she whispered to the stars.

"I do too. I remember it all. It comes back to me in dreams all the time."

"Really?" She looked at him askance. She felt him lurch and then sharply inhale. She lowered one leg to the side, but kept the other one crossing his rear.

"Well, not every time, but a lot of times. Those were good days, Amy. Crazy, but good days. I spent a lot of time being angry at you."

"I remember. I liked making you jealous."

"But I couldn't stay away."

"Yeah. And I was glad. I didn't want you to." She remembered how intensely she had felt. "You scared me. How I felt about you scared me. Like it was way too soon."

"It was too soon. Hell, we were just kids." His thumbs caressed her cheeks again. He kissed her tenderly. "Amy, you know what I mean about it being too soon?"

"Correct," she said as she pinched his nose. "Playing grownups, but not having a clue what it was all about."

She inhaled, as something hurt inside her heart. She turned her head to the right to distract herself, watching the smooth green of the course round the top of a small hill, the blades of grass shining in the moonlight. She knew she was on borrowed time.

"You okay?"

"Of course, never better." She giggled, hoping it would cheer her up more than it did.

"What's so funny?"

"I was just thinking that whenever I see a golf course, I think of these times we had. I think of you."

"Obviously you haven't taken it up."

"Never. I'd bust a gut. Honest. I couldn't do it."

Zak rolled to his back, hiking up his jeans and stared up to the stars. His hands were threaded across his chest. She folded her dress against her thigh and assumed the same position. It was a nice feeling having his warm body along the length of hers. There was something clean and honest about the way she felt, unlike before.

She could tell he'd fallen asleep so she turned carefully and watched him for a few minutes before he opened his eyes again. She wondered what he was thinking and dreaming of, if she was part of that vision.

"Sleep. I won't be getting much of it very soon now."

"Part of the training?"

"After the initial few weeks, we have Hell Week. We get like forty-five minutes sleep in five, six days."

"I know you'll make it, Zak."

"Less than ten percent chance. I doubled up on my PT before coming up here, but I've missed a couple of days."

"I believe in you, Zak. I always have."

"Thanks. I'm ready. Ready to start my life."

The comment shouldn't have hurt her, but it did. He was ready to start his life, and she wasn't really a part of it. But an agreement was an agreement, and they'd decided it would be no strings, no long goodbyes. Just a send-off.

The comforter was getting damp in the night air and despite her trying not to, she shivered. Zak immediately leapt to action, pulling one corner over her shoulder, holding it down with his long arm. She felt comfortable leaning against him, listening to the sounds of his breathing. She never wanted the moment to be over, but after several minutes she felt Zak stiffen. He uncrossed and stretched his long legs, squeezed her shoulder and said, "You ready?"

Was she ready? Hell no. But it was what she'd agreed. She'd done all the begging she would do. He was going to go off and challenge himself to do something no human had a right to think they could do. That meant that despite how she felt, she'd be strong, show him her strong side. But inside she wanted to beg him to never leave her side.

She knew the only possibility she'd get him back was if she looked like she was strong enough to let him go.

CHAPTER 7

Zak's focus abruptly shifted the first time he hit the cold water during the early phases of the BUD/S training. His swim time was good, but his running time sucked, landing him in the bottom third of the class during several initial runs. He deemed this to be unacceptable.

At night, all he could do was take a quick shower, stretch out a bit and then hit the sack. He tried not to be noticed by the instructors. Tried not to even make eye contact with others, since that one could be gone the next morning. As he looked over the class of recruits, which had dwindled down to less than half, he couldn't tell anymore who would make it and who wouldn't. He didn't even know if he'd make it or not. The only thing he thought about was not quitting.

A friend of his had to be medically rolled due to shin splints. Another recruit shattered his shoulder when one of the telephone poles came down on him. He was forced to

DOR and not allowed to return with that type of injury. The helmets lined up as the colors changed through all the phases of the training.

He'd developed a swim buddy who helped his times as they swam drag for each other and then one day, Dan just wasn't there anymore. Only thing left was his red helmet with their class number on it in white and Dan's last name: Snyder.

After BUD/S, he relaxed. The instructors still gave him trash talk, but they looked at the recruits differently. He didn't know what exactly they were looking for, so Zak decided it wasn't any of his business, he'd just stay quiet and do his job. It pissed him off when he saw a foreign trainee receive special favors from the instructors. He caught himself harboring malicious thoughts, reeling them in after hearing some of the other guys complaining too. He couldn't afford to be indignant. This wasn't the time for that.

Eventually his aloof attitude got noticed, and for the first time he felt they were looking to pick a scab. A couple of the other recruits started referring to him as the Gentleman Frog, as if he was from a privileged background.

"You got a problem hanging with the rest of us in the slime pool?" One of the recruits asked him one day. Several of the instructors looked up.

Zak had left a space between himself and the African American recruit for Charlie, who normally took that spot. He was being watched by the instructor table.

"Thought Charlie was gonna sit there. Just leaving his spot."

Recruit Carter smiled, showing a gold tooth in the front. "You see Charlie anywhere?" He motioned with his fork.

Zak scanned the room and didn't see the frizzy-haired kid he thought looked like a weasel. He shook his head.

Carter stared at the seat next to him like it had a blood stain on the bench and then back up to Zak.

Zak decided to make his comment loud enough for the instructors to hear too. "Carter, you want to cuddle, I'll cuddle with you for a bit, keep your ass warm, but that's as far as it goes," Several recruits began laughing. Carter had a piece of bread thrown at him, and the tension was broken.

Carter became one of his circle of close friends.

"I like you, white boy. You don't stick your nose where it don't belong," Carter said. "You got a past?"

"Doesn't everybody?" Zak answered.

"Oh, that they do. I'm actually lucky to be here." Carter looked out over the inlet as they sat in the sand, eating ice cream.

"Me too," Zak admitted.

"You got trouble with The Man back home?"

"Who? You mean my dad?"

"Fuck no. The Law. You have trouble with the law?"

Zak smiled and licked his ice cream.

"Oh yeah, that. That memory. I wanna know about that," Carter barked, punching him in the arm.

"Just the Chief's daughter. Lovely daughter."

"Oh snap, froglet! I'd dead if I tried that. I'm guessing her and her dad's white?"

"Yes."

"Hell, I wouldn't even try one of the black Chiefs in my home town in Louisiana. I thought you had some past." He wiped his fingers clean. "What'd you do?"

"Just pranks. Pumpkins in the pool. Jell-O in the other school's fountain."

"What the hell you talkin' about? You get arrested for throwing pumpkins and shit? I never heard about no Jell-O bandit. You bad. You a bad dude!"

Ever after that day, Zak's nickname was changed to Jell-O. Carter never let him forget he wasn't a real bad-ass, and Zak didn't want to touch what was in Carter's background. He was a fellow recruit.

He worried about what he would do to start paying his dad back, since he'd only been able to save about one thousand dollars. He didn't do much dating, and kept himself on a strict budget so he could save as much as possible, but he never could get ahead.

As the weeks went by he was so exhausted he couldn't remember even his own past, let alone anyone else's. He'd throw himself in bed at night, see another empty bed occasionally and not run to hear the story, but wait until someone told him. It just happened. People stayed. People left. That was the way it was. He had too much work to think about it anymore. He was in it until he felt like quitting, and each day didn't become that day.

Only Easy Day Was Yesterday was a suitable motto for this kind of training. He knew it would never get easier, just easier to deal with. That's why he was here.

Over the course of the next few weeks, the team bonded into a cohesive unit. Zak always deferred to others to lead, but when asked, stepped up to the plate and did his job. He never again sought out the anonymity of being a loner and he began to settle into a routine so that by the time the thirty recruits graduated, he felt like he'd die for any one of them.

His folks came down for the Trident ceremony. Over their weekend stay, he showed them what he could of Coronado. He took them to some of his favorite watering holes and noticed at every turn his dad didn't order alcohol.

"He's trying very hard, Zak," his mother told him one time while his dad was in the head. "Going to meetings, doing some light workouts. Doesn't stay down at the shop as much as he used to, and of course isn't always tinkering with that car." She stared down at her French fries.

"What did the insurance come up with?"

"Peanuts, really. He had it insured as an antique, but that didn't give him the real value to him, you know, didn't compensate for all the time he put in, and the labor he traded to fix it up. He got a check, but not enough to buy something else he felt like tackling, and way short of the real value of the car. You know how that goes. You learn from your mistakes."

"Not fair."

"Well, let's just say we'd do it differently another time, except that there won't be a next time. That was that." She looked at him hard. "Perhaps this was a good thing. Never seen him so determined to get back into shape. He's a different man when he's not drinking, Zak. I think he wants you to be proud of him."

Jack Chambers approached. "We done? Nice sunny day, good day for walking around." He put his hand on his wife's neck and gave her a peck on the cheek. It hadn't been very long ago when his dad would have preferred to stay in a darkened bar for hours on end.

Zak chose to bring up the subject of money one last time before his parents left. "Dad, I'm saving to pay you back."

His dad stared down at his feet and didn't say anything.

"Sorry to say, I've only managed to save about a grand. But it's yours. I'm giving you a check before you go."

"Nah, not necessary, Zak." Still, his dad wouldn't look at him. "Not like you have a real job, anyway. Doesn't seem right taking that from you."

Real job?

He had to say something, even if it upset his dad. "This is a real job. It's the hardest fuckin' thing I've ever done."

"I didn't mean that. I just think you need to put the past aside. You're never going to be able to pay it all back, so just quit trying. I've given up. So should you."

"But I owe you, Dad. I want to make it right."

"Forget it, Zak. You saved me from the folly of my past, in a way. Your mom will tell you I was one pissed off guy. She reminds me every day maybe I loved that car too much. Now. If you ever want to borrow another one, just for the record, the answer is no."

Before his parents left, his mother asked him if he'd had any communication with Amy. Zak told her the truth: no.

"She came by the house one day, brought me some flowers, and asked about you. I let her in. Told her you'd just made it through BUD/S and were off for your other training. We had tea. She thanked me."

"I hope you were okay with that. I haven't talked to her since the night before I left. We agreed to leave it that way, Mom."

"She looks different. She's moving to San Francisco, she said. She told me to say hi and to call her if you felt like it." His mom smiled.

"What?"

"She said she had stopped herself several times from dialing your number, because that's what you'd agreed."

"We did. What's so danged funny?"

"She said talking to me was breaking the rules a bit, but then she said you two always did break a few rules along the road."

"That's true. That's certainly true." Zak was thinking those were the best parts of their relationship.

"So I guess I'm breaking a few of my own. I told you to stay away from the Amys of the world. Now I'm not so sure about that. I think she really cares for you."

Amy didn't call him, and he wasn't going to start that up again. He needed to focus on his training. After his parents left, he tore into his studies, preparing for the underwater diving school in Florida, some jump schools, and his stint at Quantico. After that, there was talk of them doing some jungle training south of the border or back up to Alaska. He didn't care what it was. He was all in for whatever the Navy was going to shove at him.

He was proud of himself for staying unattached, because he saw how hard it was on the married guys, especially the married ones with kids at home. It changed their focus, he thought. How could it not? Right now, he knew the only time he'd be able to get more than casual with a woman was if she allowed him to have his primary loyalty to his country and to his fighting brothers. Nothing could come between him and that bond. He was grateful he didn't have to choose.

CHAPTER 8

Amy began training in San Francisco selling high-end condominiums for a large developer. The job came with wonderful perks. She got a one bedroom unit overlooking Ferry Plaza and the Bay Bridge, which included access to the exclusive gym, conference rooms for meetings with clients and a secure garage to park in.

One of her favorite walks was down the Piers, wandering through shops and boutique grocery stores where they sold hand-milled soaps, fresh-pressed olive oils and vegetables straight from the farms up north. It was an upscale farmer's market, not unlike what she was used to in Santa Rosa. Several vendors she recognized from there, including her favorite egg lady, where she bought blue and green eggs once a week.

She studied for and passed her real estate exam in the months that followed. Her father worried she was living in the City, but even he ventured to visit on a couple of occasions. One time he brought someone with him.

Marlene was a redhead with green eyes, and Amy could tell her father was totally smitten with her. She was lively, like Amy had always been. About ten years younger than her dad, she brought out some of the parts of his personality Amy hadn't seen for years. It was as if he was growing younger before her eyes. Marlene had all sorts of plans to come down and go shopping with Amy, and the idea made Amy a little uncomfortable. But as they were talking, she found herself agreeing to a future date to do just that. Her dad seemed to be delighted the two of them got along so well.

Before they left, her father ventured a private discussion with Amy. "I'm still concerned about you living down here where there are so many places you could get into trouble."

"I don't go to those places."

"But you can't avoid them. They're all around."

"Dad, you have to let go. You have to let me live my life."

"I just get so nervous thinking about you being alone here, too far away from my protection."

She kissed him. "That's sweet, Dad, but I don't need that protection now. I'm fine. This is about the safest place I could live. Honest. We have a security guard downstairs. No one comes in or up the elevators without key cards, and access to the garage is restricted."

"I know. But things can be stolen."

"Why? When there are so many other places much easier to get into? Why would they bother to rob or cause a problem here where the security is so tight?"

"I know. Probably just my active imagination." They hugged one more time, waiting for Marlene.

"She's nice, Dad. I like her."

"I do too, Amy." He stared down the hallway as Marlene's compact frame came barreling around the corner and toward them. "She's good for me," he whispered, then embraced Marlene and planted a kiss on her forehead.

"Thanks, Amy," said Marlene, her face blushing from the kiss. "I'll call you and we'll set that shopping date."

"You bet. Midweek is best for me, since I work heaviest on the weekends."

"Good for me, too. Bye."

She watched them head to the elevators, closed the tall solid mahogany door to her unit, leaned against it, and sighed. She picked up the remnants of their plates, taking them to the kitchen, and returned to her living room. Hand on her hips, she surveyed the view of the bay. She could see the smooth waters of the inlet from San Francisco to Oakland. The island to the left. The busy Ferry Plaza and Pier was teaming with tourists, even on a weekday.

The San Francisco side of the bay was still bright white, buildings looking like a bunch of folded paper cups of various sizes, anchored by tall dark spires. There was a rhythm, a pulse here. A sort of order to the way life went. She wasn't yet a part of it fully, but was stepping closer to an experience outside her control. She was partially fearful, but mostly, she was ready to join her next great adventure.

Was this how Zak felt? She wondered if he ever thought about her. On a nice clear day like today, this was something she'd like to share with him some time.

Several months later her Saturday was shattered by a stream of bright red lights and piercing sirens as paramedic vans and police cars, even a fire engine, zoomed past her glass Model Home office on the ground floor. Crowds of people began spilling out from buildings nearby, heading towards the Pier. News crews arrived and attempted to get parking.

One lone figure in disheveled green clothes, came running from the crowd that had gathered, and abruptly turned in front of her office. With his hands tucked into his jacket he lost his balance and tripped over her sandwich sign, toppling it. When he picked it up, the man's hands were bloodied, and left a bloody print on the sign as he righted it. His wild hair was pushed off his high forehead. His light chocolate skin and large brown eyes framed lips that showed a purple cast to them. He stared into the glass at Amy, his eyes full and round. He yanked on the doors, which were securely locked, waiting for her to release the button. Amy knew letting him in would be a horrible mistake.

He shook both handles, attempting to jiggle the glass, yelling something in a dialect she didn't understand, tugging and pulling on the doors in panic. He shoved against the doors with his shoulder, and although the glass bent slightly, they remained intact and didn't shatter.

Amy dialed 911, and then decided to call building security. She pushed the red button and heard a small alarm go off somewhere upstairs. The man stormed off to the left, barreling down the street, leaving a bloody print on the glass in front of her.

For several seconds Amy stared at the bloody print, frozen in place. Lights continued to flash outside, noises were escalating. She heard no shots fired and no other signs of violence or struggle. No blasts. But her eyes fixated on the red handprint with one bloody drip trailing down over the smooth clean surface of the door.

Doors behind her opened and she started, whipping around to find one building security guard entering through the rear entrance behind her, calling her name. When he reached the lobby, she noticed he was unarmed.

"I—I'm okay, but there was a guy out there with blood on his hands." Her voice was shrill. She could barely speak. Amy saw another security guard running toward the doors and stop just short, seeing the blood on the handles.

"I'll buzz him through," said the other guard as he pressed the entry button.

Amy pushed with her shoulder, letting in the second guard. "Bring in the sandwich sign," she called to him. "Don't touch where he did."

The guard reached low, bringing the sign inside the lobby, setting it down gently on the granite tile. They let the doors lock into place. A large crowd was gathering in the street over by the plaza.

"What happened?" asked Amy. "Does anyone know?"

One of the guards had been monitoring chatter on his radio. "I guess there's been a shooting at the Plaza."

"Listen," said the second guard, "I've got to help Kwon over at the Building One desk. The occupants are bound to start calling and coming home soon. You okay here?"

"Sure. You both can go. I'm safe here. Not going anywhere. I'll call the police so they can check out the blood. I'll make sure you get copied. I can let myself up to my floor through the back. I'm closing this place down."

After they left, Amy turned on her laptop and read about the shooting just being reported in the local news. Someone had shot at a military man and his wife who were taking a stroll down the Pier. His rifle had jammed after the first spray of rounds, which also caught several bystanders in the crowd. The Marine was killed by the shooter, while an accomplice stabbed the wife several times. She'd been taken to the hospital, and was now reported in critical condition.

Observers said that one assailant was dropped at the scene by one of the man's buddies, also a Marine, who was wearing a firearm. The second one got away.

Amy's stomach clenched as she realized she'd seen the face of one of the killers. She tried to remember everything about the assailant, recalling what he was wearing, what the shape of his face was.

She called San Francisco P.D. and reported what she had seen and agreed to wait until someone came by to take her statement. She shut down the lights, but remained back at her desk, following all the rushing back and forth of crowds, ready to bolt to the back if she saw someone coming toward the door. Several pedestrians walked past the doors, pointing to the blood on the handles. That certainly deterred someone from wanting to come inside the Sales Office.

News reports came in over the two hours she waited. Feeling somewhat like a fish in a glass bowl, she moved her computer and things to the kitchen area and set up at the table there, out of view of the public. Her heart was beating furiously. She knew the doors were secure but would not hold up against a bomb blast, and some on the news were reporting the backpack found had some small explosive devices in it that had remained unused.

Her cell phone rang and she jumped several inches from her chair. She thought about her dad, and cursed herself for not thinking to call him. She knew he'd be frantic with worry. She answered her phone.

"This is Detective Lombardi, San Francisco P.D. Looking for Amy Dobson."

"This is she."

"You're at the MegaOne complex still?"

"Yes."

"You reported seeing a man you think might be a suspect?"

"I don't know. His hands were bloody. He tried to come in the building, but I didn't buzz him through."

"You got a good look at him, ma'am?"

"Yes. He looked right at me."

"Okay, we're gonna send a couple guys over there and a sketch artist. Where can we find you?"

"Could you meet me at my condo? I'm up on the tenth floor. I'm getting the creeps staying down here—"

"Sorry, no. I think we need meet you there. I'll try not to make you wait longer than need be. Are you injured in any way?"

"No. And I have security I can call if I get nervous." She gave them the address of the corner Sales Office.

"We got someone over in your other lobby interviewing people. Geez, you were right there, only five blocks away." He put his hand over the phone and barked out instructions. "Okay, stay in touch with your security team and don't move. Keep your cell by you and keep it charged. We'll be over as soon as we can."

After Amy hung up, she plugged her cell into the wall socket, thanking her lucky stars for the strong WiFi signal throughout the entire building. She next called the security station and left a message she was still in the Sales Office waiting for the police. Then she called her dad.

Her father had just been told about the event in San Francisco.

"I saw him, Dad. I think I saw one of the guys."

"Hold tight, Amy, I'm coming down."

"No, don't. I'm fine. The building is very safe. The police are on their way to interview me. I don't want you down here. There are so many people all over the place, and I just—"

She finally broke down. Tears started streaming down her cheeks. She realized she'd been jumping at the sound of every siren, every flashing light coming into the lobby area. Her body was on overload.

"That's it, Amy. I'll be down in an hour. Don't go anywhere until I see you."

It didn't do any good to ask her dad to not come. She hung up the phone, sat in the dark, waiting. Her neck hurt. Her toes were cramped in the high heels she'd been wearing, so she kicked them off. She got herself a bottled water and gulped it half down before spilling it on herself. Her hands shook. Another loud peal of a rescue vehicle made her jump again.

She went into the small guest bathroom off the hallway and sat on the closed lid of the toilet and put her head in her hands. It felt good to be in the semi-darkness of that tiny room, somewhat muffled by all the noises around her. She finished the water and then stood, examining herself in the mirror. She could see the worry lines form in the middle of her forehead, her eyes were red from crying and her hair was a mess. She looked as old and tired as she felt.

A knock on the glass doors caught her attention. Two men were waiting for her, both plainclothes. She buzzed them through after she saw their badges.

"So you're Amy Dobson?" the taller one said as the doors clicked into place behind him.

"Yes."

"I'm Detective Scarpelli, and this is Mears, our sketch artist. Can we ask you a couple of questions?"

"Sure."

"Our photographer is around here somewhere, but he's a little busy."

"Can you tell me what happened?"

"Well, we're trying to put all that together. Unfortunately, we got one dead and several injured. Beyond what you hear in the news, I can't really give you anything, sorry."

"I know."

"So tell me what you saw?"

"He was a light chocolate brown-skinned man with curly hair, not real long, but curly."

"Approximately when was this?"

"Right after the sirens and things started zooming by—like within a minute after I heard the first one."

"About three-ten, then?"

"Something like that. I wasn't looking at my watch. Maybe the security guards would have a time."

"Okay, so his hair, you said it was curly?"

"Yes. Black."

"Like an Afro?"

"No, long and wavy. Maybe four inches long, just coming out all over the place. Like Garfunkle?"

"The singer?"

"Sorry, yeah. My mom always—"

"Hey, I got 'em in my family too. Hippies."

"Well, she wasn't a hippie, she just liked folk music. Anyway. Coming out like that." She gestured holding her palms all around her head.

The sketch artist began to draw. "Shape of the face?"

"Long. Thin nose, tapered. Big round brown or blackish brown eyes. His lips looked kind of purple? I know it doesn't make sense, so maybe it was the light?" she squinted.

Behind them there was tapping on the glass.

She saw a photographer taking pictures of the handles and the lobby through the glass. Another had roped off a triangle with yellow tape, keeping people away from the door.

"You wanna let him in?"

Amy buzzed the photographer and two other officers inside. They began taking pictures of the sandwich sign. Someone outside was investigating the outside glass door.

The sketch artist drew up a shape, hair, eyes. "Like this?" he said as he held up his tablet.

"Yes. Except deep, like dark colored marks under his eyes, like this," she showed them where her under eyes were puffy and red. "Darker brown, a little purple."

"Would you say he looked African, like East African, or African-American?"

"He didn't look African-American. He looked like he was from Somalia or Ethiopia. And he was thin. Very skinny. Like he wasn't from here, you know?"

After a few more questions and getting the names of the security guards, the two detectives left. Before the crime scene guys left, they took pictures of the entire space, including the hallway to the upper floor elevators outside the back door.

"We'll probably have someone posted here overnight. You have another one of these?" he said as he lifted the sign.

"Yes."

"Okay, good. Someone will be over to clean up and take down the tape. You going to be open tomorrow?"

"I—I wasn't sure I should."

"Up to you. Anything suspicious, you let me know, okay?"

"Sure."

"You got their cards too?" he said thumbing over his shoulder, indicating the two detectives who had questioned her.

"Yes."

"You call if you find anything, anything at all, okay? No matter how small."

"You—you think I should open this office tomorrow? I mean, was this a terrorist attack or what?"

"That's the thing. We don't know. All this is under investigation. More than likely it was a couple of lone wolves, just doing their thing."

Amy wasn't sure she was hearing this correctly. *Doing their thing?* Someone had been murdered. How could the world just go on its way? She must have been staring with her mouth open because the officer touched her on the shoulder, smiling.

"Look, the crime scene isn't here, so you're probably safe. You weren't the target, so why would anyone want to come back here? They were looking for big targets, crowds, in all likelihood."

"Except that he knows I saw him."

"He probably won't even remember where he ran. He was probably scared out of his mind. I mean, you think this building would be a target? With all this security?"

She recalled the conversation she'd had with her dad about it. Easier targets. Now those arguments seemed hollow.

"If it makes you feel any better, some of the shops in the Plaza are going to be open. Yes, it was a murder. But that doesn't stop life from going on. People have jobs, go to work, you know."

As the door buzzed shut behind him and he slipped under the tape outside, carting the sandwich sign wrapped in a large plastic tarp, she wondered why she hadn't heard from the building owner and developer. Or from security. No one at the complex seemed to be concerned about what had just happened to her.

She was glad her father was on his way.

CHAPTER 9

Zak and Carter were shooting darts at the Scupper. Several of the other guys joined in. They'd just gotten their orders to report to SEAL Team 3 and were given four days leave, but most of their group decided to stay around the San Diego area and get more familiar with the surroundings. Zak knew some of the guys from Team 3 hung out there regularly.

Fredo and Coop sauntered into the bar. They were most distinguishable by the fact that Coop looked nearly twice the size of Fredo. But the two were the best of friends, as they had been over the past nearly seven years together on the teams.

"Ohhh, lookie dis. We got us some tadpoles here, Coop," Fredo said shuffling over to their table. Zak had his arm extended back, ready to throw his dart, but hesitated. Fredo shook his head. "You get too distracted, my little tadpole. Never take your eye off the target."

Sure as shit, when Zak returned to focusing on the dart-board, his aim was off and the brass marker hit the wall, way off the target.

"Thought you qualified expert, Jell-O" Fredo grinned. He had a gold tooth for one of his canines.

Zak lowered his shoulders and frowned at Carter, who shrugged back in return. Several others of their group snickered.

"You like Jell-O shots?" Coop asked.

"No, sir. I don't drink."

"Smart man," returned Cooper as he looked down on the other newbies. "Fredo, they're making them younger and younger, and they're short now too."

"Another Smurf crew for sure. Thas okay. Good things come in smaller packages, right there my tadpoles?" Fredo was glad-handing all of them, slapping backs and acknowledging each one of the new guys. Coop followed as Zak hit his second and third dart, the third one right in the center.

"Look at that! A barn dart!" Coop barked. "Thought you was gonna dust them all."

"Focus. And yes, I qualified Expert," said Zak softly.

"So how'd you get the tag then, Jell-O Man?"

Zak tried to shrug it off.

"Oh come on, white boy. Tell the man," Carter shouted. "You guys gonna love this."

"I can hardly wait." Fredo came over to Zak and sniffed. "You smell like Chrome, man, that teen after shave. You don't smell like Jell-O. So what gives?"

Zak could feel his ears getting red. He figured he'd get it over with. "I pulled a prank when I was in high school. We put cherry Jell-O in the other high school's fountain. It foamed all over the place. Turned the whole quad red."

No one said anything for a few seconds. Finally Fredo turned to Carter. "That's it? Carter, what the hell you talking about?"

"No, my man!" Carter ran to Zak's side and placed his arm around his shoulder. "He got *arrested* for doing that prank. Arrested by the father of the girl he was stickin."

"Oh I get it. Daddy didn't like you and his little one hanging out, so he sort of threw the book at you?" Coop said.

Zak nodded.

Fredo gave a disgusted look by scrunching up his unibrow. "That's not funny. Carter, you got some sick sense of humor if you think that's funny. We got things way better than that and you better be ready, man. That shit," he said as he pointed to Zak, "That shit is boy scout stuff."

"I think Carter has the stories you really want to hear. Mine are just, well, probably tame," answered Zak.

"You can be as tame as you like as long as you got my six, Zak. You don't have to be outrageous to be a good team guy. You don't have to drink, don't have to do half the shit the other guys do. Just keep it clean."

"Yessir."

"Alright. So you guys are all invited over to my place tomorrow for a barbeque. You'll be on good behavior, 'cause our wives will be there. We'll invite some local girls, friends of the ladies, and such, but you be respectful. We got a few days for you to recover, but nothing stupid, and no fuckin' pranks at my house. I got two kids," Cooper boasted.

"You guys can bring your girls, if you want," said Fredo. "If they're decent type. No hookers or strippers. We got the ladies and the kids to think about."

The tadpoles grinned.

Zak's cell phone chirped. Looking down at the number, he saw it was Amy. His gut turned over as he looked at the monitor a second time.

No question. Amy was reaching out to him, and for some reason, he knew it wasn't good news.

"Excuse me for a sec." Zak ran outside and took the call on the patio which was much quieter than the inside of the bar. "Amy? That you?"

"Zak! Oh my God, Zak. I'm so glad I got hold of you."

"What's going on?"

"There's been a shooting."

Zak plugged his other ear so he could hear. His heart began to race, and his gut felt hollow. "You okay, Amy? Are you hurt in any way?"

"No, Zak, but it's like a zoo down here."

"Where did this happen? Where are you?"

"I'm in San Francisco, at my job—"

"Are you safe? Are you in a safe place right now?"

"Yes. Behind locked doors. Already talked to the police."

"So this happened at work?"

"Well not exactly. A gunman, I guess they're saying two gunmen, shot some people at the pier close to my office."

"They catch the guys?"

"No. Well, yes. One was shot, but the other one—"

"So they haven't captured everyone yet? You've got to get out of there, Amy."

"I know. I'm waiting for my Dad. I probably have to wait for the police again too. But Zak, *I saw the gunman who got away!*"

"You saw him?"

"Yes, he tried to get in the building where I work, but the doors were locked. But he knows I saw him, Zak. That's what's got me so scared. I mean I was lucky he didn't get in, but I saw his face, saw the look on his face, and he knows I would recognize him. I'm afraid he'll come back."

"You have to get out of there."

"This might sound ridiculous, but the police said I should just hold the open house like I always do on weekends. I mean—"

"That's stupid, Amy. No. You don't do that."

"It's my job. That's what I do. This just happened, so I haven't heard from the building owner yet. I'm sure he'd want to hear all about it and will probably contact me tomorrow. But I just wanted you to know."

"I'm so sorry, Amy. I didn't hear anything about this down here."

"You're back in San Diego. Not at a training site?"

"No, we just finished one set of trainings and are getting ready to do our workup."

Zak needed to make a decision and quick. He knew what would happen if he went near Amy. His overarching motivation was to help Amy feel safe, help comfort her, but he didn't want to take advantage of her fear. It was a thin line he was walking. He knew she was terrified and had nowhere else to turn, except her father, who might not be exactly what she needed right now. He felt obligated to protect her, yet knew he'd promised himself he wouldn't get entangled.

Damn. She was going to let him make the first move.

"I have a few days, Amy. You want me to come up there? Would that help?"

He heard her relax as she let out air she'd been holding. "Could you do that, Zak? I'd be so grateful." He was still shaken from the news that Amy had been so close to danger—and she was an innocent, not trained to be part of this type of action. He knew she must be working hard to hold it all together and it worried him.

"Let me see what I can do. Gotta check in with our Team liaison. I'm new to all this. If he says no, then I'll have to stay here, but I'm willing to check. The Navy owns my ass first. I'll call you back, tonight if I can." He wasn't sure how this would go over with the liaison, but he had to try.

"Thank you, Zak."

"Are you staying in San Francisco, or going home with your dad?"

"I think I have to stay here for the investigation. I just don't know. He'll want to take me home, I know. But I don't think I can. He should be here any minute."

"Okay, then. Try to get some sleep. Good that your dad's coming. I know better than to have you give him my best. Probably better you not tell him, but that's up to you."

"Not to worry. I can handle Dad. Just get up here as soon as you can. I miss you."

That was the part of the conversation that made him stumble. He'd opened the door to something bigger. Was this an honorable thing to do or a mistake? Could he trust himself?

He decided that if the Navy would let him go, he'd be there for Amy. It was the right thing to do. But not if it affected his career.

CHAPTER 10

Amy hoped Zak would be coming up. She knew it wasn't a sure thing, but took some solace in the fact that at least she'd talked to him. It settled her nerves just a little. She took a shower, letting the warm water sluice down her body, trying to put the visions of the sirens, the blood, and the killer's face out of her mind. It wasn't working.

She put on some comfortable clothes she could fall asleep in and waited for her father's text.

True to his word, Chief Allister Dobson arrived an hour plus minutes later. As usual, he pulled up to the garage gate. Amy took the elevator down and ran through the abandoned garage to where her father was parked outside the security curtain. She used her key to raise and then lower the gate after her father entered. She directed him to a spot next to her car.

Dobson took firm hold of Amy as she rushed to his arms. She felt the stiffness and tension in his frame. "Thanks, Dad," she whispered to his ear.

He seemed hesitant to let go of her, as she struggled to pull away. "Anything new?" he asked quickly. "I figured you'd call me if there was. I've been listening to the reports on the way down."

"I haven't had the nerve to watch anything except the initial reports. Waiting for you to come, I guess."

"Apparently they still haven't caught the other guy. You say you saw him?" Dobson said as they made their way to the elevators. "Who talked to you?"

Amy shrugged. "I have their cards. You can call them if you want."

"I'll do that later."

The whir of the elevator ended in an abrupt jerk as they reached the tenth floor. Amy jumped nervously and noticed her dad study her, with his eyes narrowed and a furrow between his brow.

"You okay, Amy?"

She started to tear up, grateful she was leading him down the hallway to her door so he wouldn't see her state. "I'm holding up. Just not what I'm used to."

The door closed behind her father. "No one should have to get used to this. This is what we do every day. Just can't contain all the nuts of the world. I wish it was different, but everywhere has the same problems. No one is really safe anymore. Not really."

Amy knew that now. She felt like she'd been awakened from a deep sleep. Her world of picnics, parties, hookups and shopping suddenly felt very small and meaningless. "I guess I've been living in a bubble, Dad. I just never knew how close I could be to something—"

"Now you know why I was so afraid of you living here in San Francisco. Amy, you've got to come home." Her dad looked disheveled in his dark rain slicker with two layers of shirts underneath, not the usual crisp uniform she was so used to seeing him in. He looked smaller and older than she'd remembered him.

"No, Dad. I have to stay here for now. And do you think things are really safer in Sonoma County? Really? I mean can you honestly say this type of thing wouldn't happen there too?"

Dobson angled his head. "But there at least I can keep an eye on you."

"But you protect and serve the whole community. It's your job. You can't spend your time 24/7 protecting me."

"But if you lived at home—"

"Don't you think I have to start living my own life? I mean when will it ever be safe enough?" She took his hands, drawing him over to the couch. "Sit. Can I make you something?"

"No I'm fine." Amy left him sitting in the middle of her living room as she got him some icewater. He was searching the room, looking at furniture and pictures, and then focused on the sliding glass door to the outside with views of the San Francisco skyline at night. She handed him the water, taking a seat at an adjacent chair.

"This is home now, Dad."

He took a sip and shook his head. Searching the walls and then focusing on her face, he answered her. "I don't see it.

You've made a nice place here. I can understand why you like it. Exciting to be on your own. I get that. But these are strange times, Amy. I can't even begin to tell you what we have coming in every day, alerts and information from the FBI. The whole social media thing has gotten way out of hand. We got the military asking all their service members to stay off social media, like we've been telling our own guys and gals for more than a decade now."

"Maybe it's a good thing people are more aware of their surroundings, like I've become. Although I wish it wasn't this way. I just never thought these things would happen here."

"Still the safest place around. But that doesn't mean you have to live in the middle of it. This is a nice neighborhood, and still you're not immune."

Night sounds from the city began to drain back into the background as Amy's nerves began to chill. She checked her phone, expecting either an update from building security or from Zak. It was close to nine-thirty.

"So tell me what happened, exactly," her dad asked finally. Over the next few minutes she told him about the man and her interaction with the police.

Eventually, she was talked out. The stress of the day had taken a toll on her body. "You're staying over, right, Dad? That couch makes up."

"I'll be fine. I can sleep anywhere."

"Except you're going to sleep here, in my living room. And then I'll make you coffee and breakfast in the morning. Maybe then you can check with some of your friends down at SFPD."

"Not much I can do tonight. You should check with building security before you turn in, Amy," Dobson added.

Amy did so, and was told no further incidences were recorded anywhere in the complex. She informed them she would not be holding the office open on Sunday and asked them if they'd heard from the building owners. They indicated they had not. She told them she'd been cooperating with police.

She left a message for the building management offices, who usually did not work weekends, informing them of the closed sales office.

After getting her dad situated with a blanket and pillow, she closed the door to her bedroom and climbed into bed. Her body ached. Laying her head against the pillow, she noticed her neck hurt, and her jaw felt like she'd been chewing down on something hard all day. Just before she closed her eyes, her phone beeped.

The monitor flashed a message:

'Taking an early flight to SFO. See you tomorrow. Zak.'

She texted back a smilie face, then added a heart emoticon. She'd just fallen to sleep when she heard the ping of her phone again. Zak had sent a heart as well.

CHAPTER 11

Zak raced through the San Francisco terminal, down the escalators and out past the baggage claim. He hiked the black nylon duffel on his shoulders and exited to the taxi stand, got in line and gave directions to the cab coordinator. Checking the driver's name badge swinging from the passenger window sunscreen, he noticed the gentleman's name was Addis.

"Why you want to go back down there?" Addis said as his eyes wildly searched him over the top of the driver's seat. "You hear about the news?"

"Yes. Is it still a mess there?"

"Oh, no. All quiet now. But I've been telling people to go someplace else. Pier 39, Fisherman's Wharf. Some other place. Not there."

"I'm meeting someone there."

The cabbie grunted. He swerved into the fast lane and joined the slow ribbon of steel heading into the City, several charms and a necklace hooked over the rear view mirror, flapping in the breeze of his open window. He spoke on the radio in a dialect Zak didn't understand.

He'd texted Amy that he'd landed and was on his way. It was past nine o'clock, much later than he'd expected. Now he was stuck in traffic.

"Plane was late. So much traffic," he said to the cabbie.

Addis rolled his head and then barked back, "No! Worse earlier. This is much better. Always like this on the weekend except real early. Worse on the work days. Sunshine, clouds, shootings—everyone wants to come to San Francisco today. Nuts. All peoples are nuts."

Zak was inclined to agree.

"So no word on the other shooter?"

Addis laughed. "He look like me!" He continued to chuckle, his eyes getting wide, giving a grin showing off all his stark white teeth. "But trust me, I don't know the guy. From the pictures they have, I don't know anything about him. Looks like one of thousands of peoples who live here."

Zak watched the slowly moving landscape and other passengers in vehicles. This highway had the same numbers of Mercedes as the San Diego area had. Traffic was just as bad, too.

"They're saying he was a terrorist," Zak said.

"Who knows? Somebody unhoppy. All sorts of peoples unhoppy all the time. Too many." After a pause, the cabbie looked in his rear view mirror at Zak. "You police man?"

"No."

"What you do here?"

"I'm not part of the investigation. Here to visit a friend, that's all. Visiting a—a—girlfriend."

"Okay. Well, do her a favor and take her away from this place. No place for a woman here right now."

Zak was dropped off at the front of the address Amy gave him, and he walked into the Building One lobby, after being buzzed inside by the guard behind the desk. He texted her that he had arrived.

"I'm here to see Amy Dobson. She's expecting me."

Before the guard could call up to her apartment, the back door opened, and Amy came running out. Her light brown hair was down, trailing after her. She wore faded blue jeans that hugged her impossibly thin hips, and an oversized white sweatshirt hung off one shoulder. Her fresh face sparked all kinds of good things, kicking his heart into gear as he felt adrenalin spread all over his body. Clearly, that familiar chemistry was there again. Big time.

He felt her crush into him, as his arms wrapped around her, squeezing and lifting her feet up off the floor. "So happy to see you're okay, Amy," he whispered.

"Thank you so much for coming, Zak."

They parted and he could see from the redness in her eyes where she'd been crying. "You okay?"

She slipped her arm around his waist as she waved to the guards and then took him through the doors to the hallway leading to the elevators. "Dad came last night and spent the night on my couch. He's down at the station right now, getting some information. Supposed to call me later on. I've just been here, waiting."

The elevator doors opened. Zak drew her into his arms as the elevator rose. "You must have been scared to death. What did the police tell you last night?"

"Not much of anything. Just that I should be available to them if they catch the guy. I'm apparently one of the only ones to get a good look at him. That's my artist sketch they're putting all over the news."

"Of course, you have to cooperate. I'm sure they know what they're doing."

Zak followed, holding Amy's hand as she led him to her front door. When he stepped through the tall doorway, he was stunned to see the panoramic view from coming from her sliding glass door to the outside. The San Francisco Bay, the water, the Bay Bridge and glittering buildings nearby looked like a picture perfect post card of everything beautiful about the city.

Amy walked up behind him, leaning into his back, wrapping her arms around his front. "You like?"

"My God, Amy. It's unbelievable. What a view. I don't think I've seen anything like it before."

"Yeah. I thought it was special too." She stood next to him, admiring the picture before them. She hadn't let go of his hand.

"I don't blame you," he said, turning toward her. "This is you. This is perfect for you here."

Her eyes smiled before her lips did. She stepped closer to him, putting her hands up to his neck as he laced his fingers at her lower back. "So good to see you again, Zak. Thank you so much for coming."

"Of course. Thanks for—" His lips were over hers so fast he wasn't able to finish. The traveling, the frantic phone call from last night, all his training and all the events of yesterday pushed back into the woods of his mind. It was as if they began right where they'd left off before all the drama. Before the paths they'd taken. The life they'd started separately suddenly seemed to merge into one.

He felt himself falling again down a slope he didn't want to recover from.

Amy's cell phone went off. Then it rang a second time. Amy was still returning his kisses.

"Sweetheart. Might be your Dad. The police." Zak separated them and smiled. He kissed her nose.

Amy ran to the phone. "Dad? What did you find out?"

Zak watched the slow long look she gave him, starting from his eyes, his chin and then his chest, down below his beltline, to his shoes and then slowly back up again. She angled her head in the opposite direction with a satisfied smile.

She was nodding. "So all that's good, right?"

Zak walked to the sliding glass door and walked out on the deck. Sirens didn't sound the same as they did in Sonoma County. They echoed and reverberated off the tall buildings. There was more traffic, and he was surprised to hear sounds of people talking as well as the sounds of the boats out on the water. A wind had picked up and was making whitecaps out on the blue bay.

"No, Dad. That's not necessary. I'm okay. You go on back up to Santa Rosa. I'm sure you have a lot to do up there. I'm available by phone anytime. And I'm secure here for now."

There was a pause. Zak could hear her father trying to work his way over into coming over.

"Dad. Zak came up. He's here." She paused again. "Because I called him and asked him to. After I called you. He's not staying long. I promise I'll be safe."

Some of the old stiffness returned to Zak's back and shoulders. Dobson would be not happy with this development.

"No. This isn't Zak inserting himself into my life. This is me asking for his help. This is my life, Dad. You do understand that, don't you?"

He could tell Dobson was irritated. He heard a slight edge to Amy's voice.

"No, Dad. My decision is final. He's here, and he's going to stay here for a day or two. That's all. I'll be in touch." She sighed and added, "Yes, I'll tell him." Zak heard the phone shut off.

Amy joined him at last. She slipped her arm into the crook of his elbow and leaned against him. He was going to let her tell him the message from her father. It was her story to tell. Her life. Right now, Zak was feeling like a fifth wheel, second guessing his decision to come up to San Francisco.

"No real news. But Dad said to remind you of the request he made of you to leave me alone. He said you promised."

"I did."

"But that was before all of this. Before you went off to your training. Before a lot of things that have happened since."

"Yup. He might be right, Amy."

She turned toward him, leaning back to get a good view of his entire face. "You think so, Zak?"

Zak slowly focused on her eyes, her lips, remembering the vision of her standing on the deck in the late morning sunshine. The woman he saw was different in some way. Stronger. More determined. She waited for him to respond, didn't cut him off. She *talked* to him. It didn't feel like she was pushing herself at him anymore, while he was having to spend all his time resisting her. That had been their game all growing up. Now he wasn't fighting her, he was fighting with himself.

"No. He's not right, Amy. I don't know what's out there in the future, but being here, right now, seems pretty great to me. Seems like the place I need to be."

The path to her bedroom seemed to take forever, but Zak wasn't complaining. It was the first time he'd been with her in a place of her own. It wasn't the front of his pickup or on a blanket on some golf course lawn somewhere or even at a friend's place for a stolen hour or two.

Amy faced her bed, which was shaded in the long shadows of the morning, the sun having gone to the other side of the building. Zak was standing right behind her, his palms smoothing down the backsides of her thighs as she removed her sweatshirt and turned around in her bra. His fingers gently pushed the straps off her shoulders as he held her face under her jawline and placed a sweet kiss there. His lips found the place under her ear.

She unbuttoned his shirt slowly, placing fingers against his tanned flesh, kissing him as more of his chest was revealed to her. Slowly they finished disrobing. He let her first place the condom on him, and then they slipped under her cool sheets.

Zak kissed her chest, down to her belly button and then went lower, kissing her at the top of her sex. His intense gaze focused on his fingers, now massaging her labia, pushing a finger or two inside her opening, then his thumb as he looked up at her before he bent to kiss her there.

She arched at the touch of his tongue in such an intimate spot, at the feel of his probing fingers. Her lips began to swell and she felt her pulse quicken. The sounds of their limbs shifting over the cotton sheets punctuated by the sounds of his kisses sent her into euphoria. It was all real. She could hear the sounds of the boats and the fog horns, the traffic and the bells and chimes of the city as he tasted her, as she heard his soft groan and then watched as this muscled warrior traveled up to lay against her body. They fit so perfectly together.

It was like her dream every night, what it would feel like to have Zak here with her, making love to her in her own bed on a lazy Sunday morning, as if there wasn't anything else in the world to worry about, to concern herself with. The feel of his muscled shoulders and arms was delicious as her hands smoothed up and down. The way his knees separated her thighs, pressing his groin to her core as she rose up, set her heart on fire. With her head forward, they kissed again. She would have said something, wanted to say something, but hesitated.

He spoke first. "Thank you for asking me to come to San Francisco. I wanted to see you. I should have called before—"

He rooted to find her opening as her fingers covered his mouth, and she kissed him again.

"Shhh. You're here now. It's perfect now, Zak. Truly perfect."

"Yes," was all he said as he slid inside her. He watched her face as she stared back at him through watery eyes. She closed her eyes and held her breath, feeling her breasts press against his chest as his cock filled her fully. He kissed her lids like he was begging her attention. Back and forth, their movements were long and unhurried. She studied his stubbled chin, the way his clear eyes washed her with passion, the hair falling over his forehead, the way the muscles in his back rippled as she felt the power of him.

Her body was falling in slow motion as they moved in time together. He brought her to her stomach. She placed a pillow under her abdomen as he mounted her from behind. She loved the feel of his heavy breathing at the sides of her face as he kissed her neck, elevated her hips with his hands and plunged in deep. She splayed her knees, needing more of him, not ever being able to get enough.

Slowly her orgasm built as they lay on their sides, her knee over his hip. She threw her head back as she exploded, shattering into spasms that shook her whole body. He held her hips with his hands until, side by side, she felt him pulse into her.

An hour later, they were still entangled together on the bed, hot sweat now dried. A cool breeze drifted from the living room door left open.

CHAPTER 12

Hassan shaved off most of his hair, but not his chin hair. The face that stared back at him from the cracked mirror did not look like the face on his passport. His parents even would not recognize him. If he were a woman, he could use makeup and trace his eyes, change their shape and wear something to color his lips. But this would have to do for now.

He'd hoped to receive confirmation a gift would be waiting for his parents in Aden, but nothing had come. He'd tried several numbers given to him, but no one was answering.

The news reports listed his younger brother's picture which was undoubtedly going to lead to him, since the two shared a flat in East Oakland. He doubted the baker where they worked would reveal much, if anything. Besides, all of his contacts happened at the coffee house, not at his place of employment.

He'd cleaned up at the bus terminal, washing his hands and face in the restroom filled with sleepers. The place was not a stranger to bloody handprints either. He wetted down his hair and put up his hoodie, making it over to the home of his friend, where he told him a fake story about how he'd been robbed and needed a place to crash for the night. He knew his friend worked late nights at a restaurant, so when he went to work, Hassan went on a search of things he could take with him. That's when he discovered the clippers.

His friend didn't have anything in his kitchen, except for a few pickled grains he could take. He knew he couldn't trust the man. He didn't own a television, but that wouldn't stop him from seeing Hassan's face plastered on TVs all over the city. He knew the ferries and busses had cameras, as well as some of the busy street corners. He was better off staying off the street until he could properly disguise himself.

Hassan's cell rang. After their customary greeting the voice was terse and angry.

"You dimwit."

"Did the money get sent?"

"No. You haven't finished the job."

"Sorry? The statement was made."

"Yes. But you were seen. You'll be caught."

"No. I will take my own life first. First I want to be sure my parents got the money."

"You must not be caught."

"I vow I will not be caught alive. What must I do?"

"You have to eliminate the woman who saw you."

"How do I do this?"

"You remember where you saw her. The newspaper says she worked at one of the building near the Ferry Terminal. You know it?"

"I—I don't remember very well. I could retrace my steps. But wouldn't that be risky? And the door was locked. How would I get inside the door of her office?"

"Not my problem, Hassan."

"But we have sacrificed our brother already, please."

"I'm telling you it isn't good enough. You have to make it look like they can't get away. It's the statement. You find her, you take care of it. You both go with God."

Hassan's stomach clenched. He knew he had to leave soon. Morning would bring his friend back home, and it would be too dangerous to trust him.

"You still have the devices?"

"Yes, I have three of them left."

"Good. So you find a way inside that building, you find her. I will make arrangements for the money transfer."

"But how will I know?"

"How do I know you'll do your duty?"

Hassan wanted to protest, but he knew it was a losing argument.

"You make a statement. If you get the girl, your parents get the money. No other way, Hassan. Either way, you'll be looking down from Paradise. You'll be in the garden, my friend."

After he hung up, he checked his canvas bag. The three little IEDs were tightly wrapped in plastic, then put into boxes with bubble wrap to make sure they didn't detonate before he wanted them to. He'd hold one, clutching the bag, and holding the woman by the hair, and he'd send them all away. He replayed the scene over and over in his mind. It was going to be the only thing he thought about. No reason to store up provisions, food or things to seek comfort. All this would be over in a day, maybe less. He'd have his reward, and the things of this earth—all the anger and the pain, the despair of his life—would be gone forever. It was a fair tradeoff.

CHAPTER 13

Zak woke up all of a sudden and wasn't quite sure where he was. Then he remembered their long lovemaking. He felt her warm body against him, felt the sheets tangled around his legs. Her light brown hair was all over the pillow next to him as he cradled her into his chest. How he wished he could just stay inside all day and play, stay in her arms, love her over and over again.

His forefinger rubbed along the arch of her ear, and he felt her squeeze his arm as she came to with a smile. She rolled over to face him.

"Hi," she said, looking all pink and radiant and more beautiful than he'd ever seen her. He knew a lot of things had changed, and he was seeing her colored in the light coming from his own eyes, a light that cast a rosy shadow over her and everything she was right now. This wasn't something that had ever happened to him before. He knew that he would protect her if it was the last thing he ever did.

"Amy, we have to make a plan."

"Okay, sailor. First you kiss me here," she said as she pointed to her bare right breast.

"Gladly. I intend to do much more than that, but I mean a plan about this guy, the shooter and what the police are working on."

She sat up and covered her chest with the sheet. Zak fingered the sheet down until she was sitting topless. "I like it better this way."

She leaned over and removed the sheet from his thigh and rear. "And I like it better that way."

He whipped the sheet off both of them, grabbed her and pulled her down onto the mattress again. So much for talking about a plan. Time to execute something important, something he didn't have to think about first.

Amy heated up some soup and made a small salad.

"You hear from your building owner yet, Amy?" Zak asked.

"No. I don't think they'll be in until tomorrow, but it's odd. I mean, aren't they contacted when something like this happens? Wouldn't they have precautions? I just feel like I have no guidance.

"Maybe call security?" he asked.

Zak overheard Amy's conversation with the guys at the front desk. None of them had been contacted further by the police, but they'd been pestered by news media, and several camera crews had been rushed out from the lobby after sneaking to talk to residents going and coming.

"So can't you guys get them to leave? Do they have the right to just barge in here? This is private property."

She listened further.

"Well, give the police a call, then. I think the safety of the residents is primary. And what about the owners? Any word from them?"

She shrugged, indicating to Zak the owners hadn't made contact yet.

"Who are these people?" Zak asked after she'd hung up.

"I thought they were local people, but I guess not. Overseas investors, I'm thinking. The MegaOne Group is a California corporation, but that doesn't mean all the owners live here."

"So what else did the guards have to say? Is there some protocol in place now, with all this going on? They have to have an emergency plan. It's law."

"I guess it depends on what you call an emergency."

"So how would someone sneak into the building if they wanted to?" Zak could see the suggestion was unsettling to her. "Where could you go that's safe, Amy?"

"I have no idea. My place would be safe."

"What if they knew where you lived?"

"How would he—you're not really thinking he'd come here, are you?"

"Well, let's think about it. You're living in the middle of several blocks of people who work, live and play all around you. Lots of strangers. Lots of places to hide."

"But he'd have to know what apartment I lived in. That's not posted anywhere."

"Who would know?"

"The guards. They wouldn't let anyone who didn't live here—"

Zak tilted his head to the left. "The guards? How effective do you think they'd be against terrorists? Tell me honestly, do they look like they have any military training, Amy? Honestly?"

"Well, no."

"Exactly. So what do you think?"

"It's a big assumption. You assume he'd go to the trouble to find me, where I live. I just don't think the world works that way. Maybe in the movies. But in real life? Do you honestly think he'd be stupid enough to come back here, knowing I could recognize him?"

"We're not talking about fantasyland, Amy. This is the real world. So humor me, where would you go if you couldn't come here?"

"There's a theater. A public kitchen. Some conference rooms."

"Okay, the kitchen would have knives and things. Good. A conference room?"

Zak shook his head. "No. You ever try to beat someone up with a wastebasket or a phone?"

"I'm not trying to beat someone up. Besides, I'll have you here."

"You own a gun?"

"Fuck no."

Zak was actually sorry she didn't.

"Illegal in San Francisco."

"Which is why the shooting happened here, my guess."

"Did you bring one, Zak?"

"No. I left all that behind. Not sure that was so smart."

Amy took their dishes to the sink. She turned around. "I guess the gym on the ninth floor, just below us, would be safe. He'd need a key card to get in." She showed him the ring with her two key cards on it. "I keep one here at all times, the other one goes with me everywhere."

"So he'd steal one."

"The gym has some places to hide, maybe. Some hand weights and equipment, maybe. Ropes. What do you think?"

Zak stood up and gave her a hug. "That's my girl."

The security desk called and asked Amy to come down to pick up a form the owners had faxed into the guard station and wanted her to fill out. At about the same time, Zak got a call on his cell from San Diego. He began updating his liaison on the situation and confirming he arrived safely as Amy grabbed her card and held her finger up.

"Wait, I'll go with you," said Zak as he cradled the phone.

"No. We have no reception in the elevators. I'll be right back."

Amy was out the door before he had time to protest. He finished his call and sat back. He knew he'd just screwed up letting her leave.

CHAPTER 14

Amy hadn't even bothered to put her shoes on. She was running down the hallway in the flip-flops she kept by the front door. She almost turned around to go back to the apartment, but changed her mind as the elevator doors opened.

She flipped the key card back and forth in her palm. The conversation with Zak was troubling, but she knew why he wanted to have it. His brief time in the military made him wary of all sorts of dangerous situations. That was a good thing. One couldn't be too careful, she thought.

Zak's being present had a levitating mood on her spirit. She was sure he was as into her as she was into him. This morning and early afternoon had opened up a new phase in their relationship, something she wanted to explore fully. Sure, the passion and the fire was still there, but now there was something else. Something—

She heard noises on the other side of the doors leading to the guard station in the lobby. Just as she opened the door, she heard a scream. A woman was jammed in the glass door-way of the building, halfway inside, halfway outside. She'd dropped her purse and her eyes were wide as she looked in panic at Amy's face. She screamed again.

Then Amy noticed that at her side was a man, the same man she'd seen in the doors yesterday, wearing the same green khaki clothes, although his appearance had changed. But there was no mistaking the murderous stare he fixed on Amy as he held something up to the woman's neck. A wide ribbon of dark red blood was trailing down her neck, over the man's hand, onto her shirt, and spilling onto the floor. Her legs were pumping back and forth, slipping in the red goo as she struggled to stand up.

The lone security guard was on the phone before the man dropped the woman on the floor with a loud thud, ran over to him and yanked the phone from the guard with his bloody hands. Another man rattled the glass doors and began to shout.

Amy turned and ran. Luckily, the elevator was still at the bottom floor and as she pushed the button, she noted the stairs and swore under her breath, instead wishing she'd made that choice. As the doors closed, she gasped in relief.

She tried to text Zak, but her lack of cell reception made that impossible. The elevator stopped on the fifth floor, with a couple wanting to get inside.

"Call 911. There's a break-in down at the security office," she shouted to the older couple who jumped at her words.

As the elevator headed to her floor, she heard the security alarm system sound, asking residents to evacuate the build-ing. It took forever for the elevator to make it to the tenth, and she ran down the hall to her door, pounding against it.

"Zak!" she shouted. No one answered. She inserted her card and stormed into the room. Zak wasn't anywhere. His duffel bag still sat at the foot of the bed. Dishes were still in the sink. She called out for him several more times, even going out onto the deck. Adrenaline was pumping through her so fast, she thought her heart would burst.

Out on the balcony, she dialed him. The line was busy.

She continued to call but knew the rapid busy signal was probably generated from multiple people trying to call out. At the kitchen she stopped. The hook that hosted her key cards was now empty. She had one. That meant Zak had the other. He'd taken the card and gone after her.

"Fuck!" she screamed. Outside she heard a siren. She dialed 911 and got another busy signal.

All of a sudden she remembered their conversation this afternoon. Opening the door, she glanced down the empty passageway with the door to the exit stairs four doors down. Several residents were beginning to come out of their rooms. She carefully closed her door, leaving her flip-flops in the hall. She didn't want them slowing her down or making slapping noises while she ran.

Barefoot, she slipped past a cluster of residents waiting for the elevator. She quietly opened the heavy metal door to the stairwell getting the attention of a couple other residents who began to follow her. She quietly ran down the metal grids until she got to the entrance of Floor 9. The doorway was closed, but unlocked. She could hear other residents heading down the stairs from below and someone running up, pushing past other people moving opposite.

She poked her head over the railing, hoping perhaps it was Zak, and came face to face with the shooter, staring up at her from two landings below. Immediately she ran through the Floor Nine entrance, nearly toppling as she banged against the walls. She passed utility and equipment room signs, as well as a unisex bathroom, until she found the glass doors of the gym. Quickly scanning her key card, she went inside the cool studio dotted with weight equipment and matting. As the glass closed behind her she heard the stairwell door burst open, followed by footsteps.

Amy chose to run into the men's rest room, thinking he'd not expect that. She stood on the black seat of the toilet, trying to keep the metal stall opening from swinging back and forth, and held her breath. She was gripping the key card so tight it nearly cut into her palm, so she quickly inserted it inside her bra.

Listening for every sound, she heard someone swipe the key card and walk inside the gym. Their deliberate steps were calm, unhurried.

"I have captured you. It is of no use to run," the man shouted. She could hear him chatter prayers while he searched. "Your days of living a filthy life in a filthy country are over forever. It is no use holding out for a chance at what you call redemption. This is your fate."

Amy heard chanting as the man began to sing a prayer, repeating a stanza several times over and over again. That's when she realized he wasn't going to come after her, but was going to do something else instead.

She tried to recall what the news reports had said. The first shooter had with him several small explosive devices which had been undetonated, indicating he'd been stopped before they could achieve their original goals.

She looked at the metal walls of the lavatory stall and hoped it could save something of her—enough so she might survive a blast. She put her head below her outstretched arms, resting her chin on her knees as she attempted to squat and balance on the flange of the toilet, and held her breath.

She thought about her dad and mentally told him he was right, telling him she was sorry she hadn't listened. She thought about Zak, his kisses, the way he'd loved her body for hours throughout the middle of the day.

If there ever was a perfect time to die, let it be on a day like today. A beautiful day, full of love. Loving someone who loves me back completely.

She felt the hot tears form at the tops of her cheeks at the injustice of it all, knowing Zak would do what he could to avenge her. She prayed that he didn't wind up being too bitter and angry, that he keep working for the good and decent people of the world.

She took one last, long breath and then heard the sound of a key card on glass, the doors pushed open, and a struggle on the mats in the other room. Something metal hit the ground. Someone grunted.

Amy jumped off the toilet, picking up a wooden plunger she found sitting on the granite tiled floor next to a waste basket. As she rounded the corner she saw Zak wrestling with the shooter as they rolled over the mats in a life and death struggle. Running up to the clutch of arms and legs, teeth and blood from bites and scratches, she raised the plunger and with all her might forced it down on the shaved head of the shooter, breaking the wooden stick in splinters.

Zak looked up at her stunned, his eyes round with fear. He grabbed the sharp stump end in her hands, and stabbed the shooter in the chest, forcing the wood through a crunching of ribs and bone. Blood spurted up like a fountain, covering them all. Zak pointed to the corner.

"IED."

The little metal tube was still rolling until it hit the outer wall, near a large plate glass window. In slow motion, Amy felt the tug on her arm as Zak pulled her through the glass doors and began running down the hall. A second or two later, a huge explosion blew out the glass doors, sending large shattered plate glass like a wave over the whole floor.

Zak tackled her, covering her completely and they slid to the furthest corner away from the gym doors just as another larger explosion sent a fireball that ignited the carpet and the walls and caused the metal light fixtures to melt and drop like candy syrup.

As things began to pop, explode and drop all around them like a mechanical rain, she listened for signs of life coming from the body shielding her. Smoke in the air made her cough. Sprinklers began hissing and attempting to shoot water in uneven sprays over everything. She was lying on her stomach and something was beneath her, pressing against her abdomen. And then it moved. One of Zak's arms was slowly trying to move to the side as another arm held her forehead from pressing into the floor. She felt his warm breath in her ear and heard the delicious sound of his voice, "Are you okay, baby?"

"Yes. How about you?"

He groaned and said through parched lips, "I think I broke a couple of ribs, but I'll live."

She started to lift herself up onto her elbows, as Zak sat up, pulling her up with him. "Does that hurt, sweetheart? Can you sit?"

Turning her body, Amy saw his roughed up face, including a couple of head wounds. His blue eyes sparkled back at her, dancing in the light of the small fires surrounding them. She gingerly kissed his cut lips as water streamed down his face.

"Amy, I think this is what you'd call explosive chemistry," his voice husky.

She laughed, hugging him until he seized up again, knees coming up to his chest when she squeezed too hard.

"Sorry. Sorry, Zak. I forgot."

"Sure you did, kid. You've always been the one to get me into trouble. Look at this place. You think they'll fire you?"

She laughed again. "Ask me if I care."

"Anything hurt?"

"My head," she reached behind and felt a knot Zak found as well." Her hands were covered in cuts, and she was beginning to show signs of bruising. Zak helped her up to standing position.

Another light fixture crashed to the ground, and she started. She could hear sirens and the blare of large rescue vehicles and possibly fire trucks sounding a long ways down below. Wind whipped through the hallway tunnel, blowing fabric, and pieces of miniblinds that bundled up looking like metallic bunches of grapes.

Zak had a trickle of blood falling down below his ear. His lips were cut and chapped, and he squinted. A large purple welt was forming on the right side of his forehead.

"The shooter?" she asked.

"Oh, they'll find bits and pieces of him all over this floor, probably scrape some of him off the side of the building too when the window washers come." Zak coughed. "We should get out of here. Can you walk?"

She tried a step, her arms around his waist. "I'm good."

"Let's get out of Dodge," he whispered, leading her toward the stairwell entrance. He pushed her behind him as they walked past the nonexistent doors to the gym and found the windows had completely blown out, the force of the blast overturning equipment. The mirror-covered walls covered in blood spray looked like a contemporary painting. Several rags of clothing remnants soaked in deep red puddles against the walls. There was a large crater blasted in the center of the room with splinters of flooring scattered everywhere like toothpicks.

Opening the stairwell door, they could hear heavy boots running up the steps, carrying equipment. "Anybody up there injured?"

"We're fine. Not sure about anyone else, but I think your shooter has become one with the source," Zak barked.

CHAPTER 15

The oyster bar at the Ferry Plaza he had on good authority was a good place to have a special occasion. His new LPO for SEAL Team 3, Kyle Lansdowne, had told Zak all about it, told him to say his goodbyes and then get his butt back to San Diego for the workup.

"You don't want to start out on this team as a slacker. We don't really get time off, so while it's nice to get all cozy with the girlfriend and get her head on straight, we've got a mission to work up for."

"Roger that, sir."

"We can't always come home. Most of us miss holidays, anniversaries, kid's birthdays, and even our kid's births on a regular basis. That's just the way it is. Don't cry over it."

"I get you, sir."

"But damn, I gotta say for a little tadpole, a newbie frog, you sure handled yourself well, sailor. Way to get that little punk to give it up and not take any more people with him."

"Thank you, sir."

"Mighty proud. And your lady, I hear tell she held up quite well. You got a keeper there, son."

"I think so too, sir."

"So what the fuck you waiting around for? Ask the girl to marry you, and get her little ass down to San Diego where you can keep an eye on her."

"I intend to, sir."

"I'm gonna ask you first thing when I see you next. Don't complain and cry on my shoulder telling me you screwed all night long and forgot to ask her, okay? Make an honest frog princess outta her, son."

"I get your message loud and clear, Chief Petty Officer Lansdowne."

Amy was returning from the ladies room, so he signed off and took a sip of his beer. She sat next to him. Except for the fact that the two of them looked like they'd gotten into a fight, Zak thought they made a pretty good looking couple as he stared across the bar to the large wavy mirror. The waiter brought them six barbequed oysters from Marin County. The hot spicy tomato flavor wafted up in the steam that blew in their faces as they hovered over them.

"Those look wonderful." Amy's eyes were bright, her face illuminated by soft candlelight.

Zak squeezed a lemon wedge over the hot mixture. He held one shell up to Amy's mouth. "Yours. These are supposed to be the best in the bay."

Amy swallowed the mixture, shutting her eyes as a little part of the sauce dribbled out the right side of her lips. Zak kissed it away.

"Your turn," she said and held up another shell, tipping it so the hot oyster mixture slid onto his tongue.

"Hog Island is famous to SEAL Team 3, or at least to our LPO."

"LPO? What does that mean?"

"Leading Petty Officer. He's like in charge of our platoon. You'll get to meet him soon, I hope. Maybe there will be time before we deploy, but for sure when I get back."

"So what are your dates?" She asked, taking another oyster.

"Well, that kinda depends on you, Amy."

"On me?"

"When I come home next time, I'd like to ask your father permission to marry you, if you'll have me."

Her smile started slow, and for a second Zak panicked. But when her lips turned up and she winked at him, he relaxed. He'd been nervous all day, knowing he wanted to ask her, and not knowing exactly how to do it, until Kyle told him about this place. And it seemed fitting to do it here, near where all the violence had happened, where their lives had changed forever.

"If you can't answer, I'd totally understand. You don't even know about the community, and it's not an easy life. Hell, I'm just getting used to it myself, getting to know all the guys. But these are special guys, unlike anyone else I've ever met. I think you'd fit right in, if you're willing."

"Of course I'm willing. You sure, though?"

"Completely. You wanted to be the girl I came back to. I want that too."

She looped her arm through his and leaned into him, rubbing her chest against his elbow. "So did you ever think of a Plan B? I mean, what if I said no?"

"Well, I was going to go look for a golf course."

The End

If you enjoyed this novella, please read the revised and expanded full length version of Zak and Amy's story, coming out in November 2015, Book 1 of the True Blue SEALs Series, True Navy Blue.

For other information about all of Sharon Hamilton's other books in her SEAL Brotherhood Series, or her other books, please go to her website: authorsharonhamilton.com. You can find out about her schedule, new releases, her audio books, as well as sign up for her newsletter or join her street team. She likes to stay in touch with readers, so feel free to leave her an email at: sharonhamilton2001@gmail.com.

OTHER BOOKS IN THE
SEAL BROTHERHOOD SERIES:

BOOK 1

BOOK 2

BOOK 3

BOOK 4

BOOK 5

BOOK 6

BOOK 7

BOOK 8

BOOK 9

ALL AVAILABLE ON KDP & AUDIBLE!

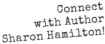

ANTHOLOGIES:

SEALed With A Kiss

Paranormal Romance
Super Bundle

Romancing the
Military Man
Anthology

To Protect
and Serve
Anthology

OTHER BOOKS BY SHARON HAMILTON:

The Guardians Series

BOOK 1

BOOK 3

BOOK 2

ALL AVAILABLE ON KDP & AUDIBLE!

The Golden Vampires of Tuscany Series:

BOOK 1

BOOK 2